PRAISE FOR LIA MATERA
AND HER WILLA JANSSON MYSTERIES

"A right snappy storyteller."
GREGORY MCDONALD

"What a refreshing young sleuth! Characters keep me coming back to an author, and I hope to see these again soon."
JULIE SMITH

"Willa Jansson is a pleasure to meet, and her wryly humorous view of contemporary society makes for extremely entertaining reading."
MARCIA MULLER

"Matera has her own distinctive voice."
The San Diego Union

"Willa Jansson is a delightful narrator."
Drood Review

HIDDEN AGENDA

Lia Matera

BALLANTINE BOOKS • NEW YORK

Copyright © 1988 by Lia Matera

All rights reserved under International and Pan-American Copyright Conventions. Published in the United States of America by Ballantine Books, a division of Random House, Inc., New York, and simultaneously in Canada by Random House of Canada Limited, Toronto. Originally published by Bantam Books in 1988.

Grateful acknowledgment is made for permission to reprint the lyrics from "DO YOU LOVE ME?" (Sheldon Harnick, Jerry Bock) © 1964—ALLEY MUSIC CORPORATION and TRIO MUSIC COMPANY, INC. All rights administered by HUDSON BAY MUSIC INC. Used by permission. All rights reserved.

The law firms and business institutions depicted in this novel are imaginary. So are the lawyers, bankers and other characters. Any resemblance they may bear to actual individuals or institutions is purely coincidental.

ISBN 0-345-37128-3

Manufactured in the United States of America

First Ballantine Books Edition: March 1992

To Ennio—the best of all possible brothers.

1

It began with a phone call at seven in the damned morning. I could hear the buzz of long-distance cable. "This is Willa Jansson," I admitted grudgingly.

"And this is Thomas Spender!" His tone said, *Bully for me!* "We met in January of your last year of law school."

I frowned down at my bare toes, kicking aside some underwear. If he was waiting for me to say "How nice," he would wait a long time. My last year of law school was not a cherished memory.

"In the midst of that, um . . . imbroglio."

Imbroglio—The word crackled across my sleepy synapses. I remembered somebody using that word, somebody from—"Wailes, Roth—"

"—Fotheringham and Beck. Yes, indeed. You remember our interview!"

Despite plans to work for a respectably radical law firm in San Francisco, I'd interviewed with two morticians (that's what they'd looked like, anyway) from an

1

august Wall Street firm. Thomas Spender, Esquire, began to take shape in my memory: plump and pinstriped, the spawn of some Republican Central Committee petri dish.

"Let me get to the point, Ms. Jansson. We, uh, heard that your law firm—I believe you worked for Julian Warneke's firm?" He spoke the name with bemused contempt. "And that firm is now, uh, somewhat defunct?"

Somewhat defunct—the murder of two partners and a secretary will do that. "The firm doesn't exist anymore," I confirmed. Anyone who read the newspaper knew that.

"The reason I mention it is, I find we still have your law school résumé on file. And we, um, thought you might care to send us an *updated* vita."

I edged closer to my bedroom window and pulled up the shade, flinching from the morning light. I was surrounded by laundry, books, papers, dust balls: it was my room, all right. Not a dream.

"Send you an updated résumé?" Since when did the biggest, piggiest law firm on The Street have to *solicit* résumés? And why from me? I'd done well in law school, but Malhousie wasn't a top ten school. And Wailes, Roth was the kind of firm that Stanford and Yale Law grads grovel before, after clerking at the Supreme Court.

"Let me tell you what made us think of you, Ms. Jansson. In spite of the publicity about the Warneke, um—" I guessed he didn't want to use the word imbroglio again. "That was rather unfortunate, of course, but—Tell me, do you know Bud Hopper?"

"No."

"Jolly decent fellow." The Manhattan accent was temporarily anglicized. "Apparently a very high muck-a-muck in the Department of the Interior. He has the President's ear, you might say."

"The one with the hearing aid?"

A slight pause. "Oh yes, huh huh. Anyway, Bud has some friends in the INS—Immigration and Naturalization—"

"I know what it stands for."

"Of course you do!" He spoke with walrus-to-the-oysters heartiness. "I understand you wrote an excellent little law review article about alternative immigration restriction scenarios."

"My student article?" In which I did *not* use the word "scenario." Not once.

"Bud tells me some very senior White House aides looked at that article. In fact"—his tone was both superior and congratulatory—"Bud tells me the President's people even kicked around one or two of your thoughts when they made their limited amnesty recommendation to Congress."

I almost groaned. The latest Republican plan allowed bosses to continue exploiting their existing cheap foreign labor, while slamming the door on future immigration. "I'm sure you misunderstood your friend—"

"Now, now. No false modesty! I haven't had a chance to peek at the article myself, but Bud Hopper certainly seemed to think it was a good piece of student work." He added brightly, "Good enough for the Reagan administration!"

I sat down, almost missing the edge of the bed. Lately I'd been pining over a cop; if my parents learned I'd also contributed, however unwittingly, to the Republican body politic, they would wander the streets in sackcloth and ashes.

"And," he continued, "a few of the partners here were sufficiently impressed when I mentioned it to suggest that I call you this morning and invite you to update your résumé."

"Mr. Spender, thank you. But I don't think I'd like to move to New York."

"No, no, Ms. Jansson. It's our San Francisco office that needs a new associate."

"I didn't know you had an office here."

"A recent addition to our, um, constellation. Quite small, for the time being—an extension of our Los Angeles office, really. Two partners and four associates, but we plan a very accelerated expansion. And naturally, we would be prepared to lateral you in."

I briefly considered the verb. Was it better than being verticaled? "Lateral me?"

"Give you credit for your two years with the Warneke firm."

"In what sense?"

"Salary and seniority," he said indulgently. "I believe our third-year people are making about ninety thousand. It goes up quite sharply in the fourth year, and continues climbing until one makes partner in the seventh year, assuming one does. Partners, of course, are on a different scale altogether."

Ninety thousand dollars! And goes up sharply! Warneke, Kerrey, Lieberman & Flish, the law firm of my left-wing dreams, had been paying me twenty-five five before becoming somewhat defunct.

"Let me give you the name of a contact person in our San Francisco office," Spender continued, in the same indulgent tone. "In case you decide to give us a call."

And, with the breathless obedience of a Nancy Reagan, I purred, "Let me get a pencil!"

2

"MOTHER," I HEDGED, watching her turn the crank of a mimeograph machine Gutenberg would have shunned. "I think it's important for women to assume their rightful positions in the power structure. Don't you?"

Her varicosed legs moved rhythmically back and forth as she cranked out smudgy copies of her latest tract. She wasn't really listening; in our family, liberal sentiments are white noise.

I kept trying. "Especially since"—since what?—"it's almost an election year."

Mother stopped cranking and pulled the topmost copy off the stack. Her fingers were stained purple, and her mouth pursed as she scanned the tome. It had come out crooked, as usual. From what I could see, it announced the formation of yet another People's Media Alliance.

"So I've joined a new firm," I concluded, rather forlornly.

" 'Manipulate the media!' " Mother read aloud.

5

When the Yippies had their twenty-year reunion, my gray-haired mother would be standing in line at the punch bowl.

"I've joined a new law firm, Mother."

She blinked. "A new firm? Legal Aid? Charles Garry?"

"Not exactly." How to break the news that I'd be representing banks and holding companies instead of migrant workers and labor unions? "But I did get the job because of that immigration article I wrote."

Mother's blue eyes lit with pride. "The Agricultural Labor Relations Board! That's *wonderful*, Baby!"

"Well, no. What I was saying before about women joining the power elite. . . . " I looked around the under-furnished, cushion-scattered Haight–Ashbury flat. From every wall, posters urged me to Feed the Hungry and Learn the Lessons of Vietnam. I sighed. "The firm's called Wailes, Roth, Fotheringham and Beck."

Mother looked uncertain: Judeo–WASP names, all— no named partners of color. Could I persuade her Wailes was an African tribal name? "What kind of law—?"

"It's definitely a power structure kind of firm, Mother." Seeing her jaw drop, I hurried on. "But the point is, it's been a bastion of the old-boy network for fifty years and I think it's time women began to . . ." *Make a lot of money*, I concluded silently.

Mother put down her tract, ostentatiously straightening her spine. It always meant trouble when she remembered her yoga. "Did *he* put you up to this?"

He had not returned my phone calls for two months. Not since the Civil Service Commission had verbally censured his conduct in a murder case—the murder of my former boss, Julian Warneke. The complained-of conduct had been, at least in part, an errand of mercy on my behalf: San Francisco Homicide Lieutenant Don Surgelato had shot and killed an unarmed murder suspect. If the "suspect" (read "murderer") had lived, my mother's association with an underground organization would have been revealed. She'd have ended up in jail.

Not that Mother minded going to jail; it was something she did now and then, to catch up on her correspondence with the Berrigans.

I was the one who hated to see her behind bars; and my gratitude toward the lieutenant (unexpressed, because he would not return my phone calls) stopped just short of disconsolate love.

San Francisco's legal establishment had a different reaction. Led by my former criminal procedure professor, it now rancorously lobbied for the lieutenant's suspension from the force.

And my mother, damn her, had personally organized two "Suspend Surgelato" rallies on the Hall of Justice steps.

"*He* has probably never even heard of Wailes, Roth, Mother!" I restrained an impulse to screech at her—I didn't need another baleful lecture on the family *chakra*. "I'm just sick and tired of—"

"Your moral principles?" Outrage glowed on her finely wrinkled cheeks.

"Rotten pay! Legal Aid, the ACLU, and Ag Board— they don't pay enough to keep you in bus fare in a city like San Francisco! I'm sick of being underpaid! And I'm sick of being told I'm lucky because there are a hundred lefties out there drooling over my job!"

"Money!" She might have been saying "rat poison!" "Willa June, there's a great deal more to life than—What about helping your fellow human beings? Don't you believe—"

"There'll be pie in the sky when I die?" I reprised my only ideological argument: "Women have to start infiltrating the power structure, Mother!"

For a moment my mother, very much in the habit of approving my actions, seemed to waver.

Unfortunately, my argument was transparently self-serving. Mother might be a bleeding heart, but she was no dummy.

"Oh, Wiiiilla!" she moaned. "You've *sold out*! I never, *ever* thought it would happen to *you*!"

And she crossed herself, in silent prayer for my radical soul.

3

WILLIAM K. MOTT was compact and funereal, with black hair brushed straight back, and a long, frown-creased face. He wore a midnight blue suit, a white shirt and a burgundy tie. He carefully unfolded a pair of horn-rimmed half glasses as he squinted down at my résumé.

"Malhousie," he murmured with mild distaste. Merely Malhousie (as it was sometimes called) was at the bottom of the list of "better" law schools, right after Minnesota. Good enough, but not top drawer. Not

Stanford, Harvard, or Yale—but not Temple, Memphis State, or People's College, either.

For ninety thousand a year, I could bear to hear my alma mater disparaged. "I was in the top five of my class. And a Stanford undergraduate." And then, because Mott continued to look unimpressed: "I was also acting editor-in-chief of law review for a while." I felt a stab of guilt; at the time, I'd scorned the fervid ambition of those seeking that position. It had become mine only through mishap and inadvertence.

Half glasses settled low on his nose, Mott continued examining my résumé. I looked nervously around the office. It was decorated in gray, navy, and plum with abstract landscapes in matching shades. Behind Mott was a framed photograph of Gerald Ford that might have been labeled "What, me worry?" On his desk was a tidy stack of files beside an open briefcase. His gray leather office chairs probably cost more than my former boss's entire five-office suite. Behind Mott, wall-to-ceiling windows overlooked the colorful bustle of the financial district. Coit Tower, glamorously spotlighted, rose in the background. My old office had a view of a parking garage.

Mott finally commented, "Top five; editor-in-chief; mm-hm, mm-hm. And of course the article Bud Hopper mentioned. Tell me, what kind of work did you do for Mr. Warneke?"

"Litigation." I was glad to focus on what I'd done—not who I'd done it for. "Law and motions, primarily; but also depositions, administrative hearings, contract negotiations—"

He glanced up from the résumé. "Any trial experience?"

"One jury trial," I admitted reluctantly. He wouldn't approve of the cause of action; and besides, I'd lost the case.

"Second-seating Mr. Warneke?"

"No." I could feel myself shrink deeper into the leather. "This was shortly after his, um . . . death."

"Ah, yes." He frowned at my résumé again, fumbling with the buttons of a space-age telephone. A moment later, a Lauren Hutton clone glided into the office. "Robert will want to see Ms. Jansson next, I think, Jaclyn." Mott tilted his chair backward, lacing his fingers on the desk top. As I stood to leave, he explained, "I maintain this office for my occasional jaunts north, but my primary locus is the Los Angeles office. Robert LeVoq"—he smiled weakly—"is actually the senior partner in this office." He added grimly, "I am the *managing* partner!"

He and Jaclyn exchanged a glance that fizzed like damp fireworks.

4

Robert LeVoq was talking into his speaker phone, feet on his desk, a pad full of geometric doodles before him. He looked to be in his midthirties—my age. He had blow-dried brown hair and pockmarked, chip-

munky cheeks that added to a first impression of boyish charm. He wore a daringly pale suit with patterned
socks of the same shade and a big, sporty watch. There
was a frat boy sparkle in his close-set eyes.

"Marty, Marty! No way!" he bellowed in the direction of his speaker. He waved me into the office, glancing first at my breasts, then at my legs, then at my hair.
He nodded approvingly: a cute little blonde. (He would
learn different, if he hired me.) "We're ready to go on
this one right now!"

A New York Jewish voice crackled from the speaker.
"Bobby, what the hell difference does it make to you?
If you're ready now, you'll be ready next month! *If*
you're ready now!"

"Ready!" "Bobby" laughed, a rolling chuckle that
sounded rehearsed. "Tell your client to enjoy the Mas-
erati while he can still afford it, buddy! And forget the
continuance!" LeVoq winked at me as I sat opposite
him. "Look at it this way, Marty—your wife'll have a
better time in Italy without you!" He clicked a button,
terminating the call. "*We* don't take vacations—why
should they?"

No vacations? I hoped he was kidding. "I'm Willa
Jansson. Mr. Mott sent me."

He pumped my hand, holding it a trifle too long and
glancing again at my breasts. "Bob LeVoq! Sit down.
Jackie," he said to the Lauren Hutton clone, "wait a
sec!"

While LeVoq stacked the scatter of file folders on his
desk, I looked around. The office was almost as big as
Mott's. It was done in cream, black, and red, accented
with abstract torso sculptures of big-hipped women. It
too had a view of Coit Tower.

LeVoq handed Jaclyn the stack of files. "Give these
to Melinda, would you? And tell her we're still on calendar with Transport Trust."

Jaclyn took the stack, a slight frown on her model-

perfect face. Seeing it, LeVoq chuckled again. As Jaclyn turned to leave, he leaned across the desk and extended his arm as if to pat her fanny. At the last second,
he flicked a crumpled ball of paper off his desk instead.
And laughed.

"Sooooo." His voice made the transition to busi-
nesslike. "Tell me about your last case."

Damn. "I defended a boy who refused to register
with the selective service."

LeVoq's plump-cheeked face showed neither ap-
proval nor disapproval; he looked, in fact, sincerely ea-
ger to discuss it. "What were the legal issues?"

"Whether a violation of the Selective Service Act can
be justified by a moral objection to—"

"*Legally* justified? There's a clear statutory duty to
register with the selective service at age eighteen! Period!" His voice boomed, his hand waved: he was rev-
ving into litigator mode. "If you don't register, you're
in clear violation!"

"The statute doesn't allow for individual gestures of
conscience, that's true—but juries do, sometimes."

LeVoq laughed, obviously enjoying the discussion
more than I was. "So you're saying there was no way
you could have won on the merits? But you went ahead
anyway!" He sat forward, crossing his arms atop a stack
of file folders. "You know, Willa, I always tell my people: To hell with the merits! If the facts are against you,
argue the law. If the law's against you, argue the facts!
Who'd you appear before?"

"Judge Rondi." I tried to suppress a shudder.

LeVoq snickered; apparently he'd appeared before the
old fascist, too. "Oh well, it shouldn't matter who
you're up before! What matters is—" He looked over
my shoulder, a sly, almost contemptuous gleam in his
eye. "Melinda! Meet Willa!"

I swiveled in my chair. A tall woman in a blue-
trimmed black suit was standing at LeVoq's office door.

Her shoulder-length brown hair had bowl-cut bangs, and her face, like mine, was makeup free. She appeared capable of intelligent good humor—her mouth, showing a considerable overbite, had laugh lines around it. But right now, her straight brows were pinched, and her jaw was clenched. "Have you done *anything* on Transport Trust?"

"Get back to me tonight. We'll brainstorm," he replied airily.

Melinda weighed a hefty stack of file folders on her palm. "Sixty pages of interrogatories, a document production request that's going to send Transport through the ceiling, and one day left to file a motion to quash." She slapped her other hand on top of the files. "I've been asking for *months* if you want me to take over this case! What's the point of turning it into a paper war, anyway? I thought you were going to phone Marty and settle out."

"He just asked me to stip to a continuance." The sly gleam returned to LeVoq's eyes. "I figured, hell, if *he's* not ready—! It gives us an advantage! We'll be ready in time, don't worry!"

"We? What are *you* doing tonight, Bob?"

He smiled sweetly. "You can reach me at home if you have any questions."

She flushed in unattractive splotches. Her lips moved soundlessly. If my lip-reading was correct, the self-censorship was entirely appropriate.

"Say hello to Willa!" LeVoq suggested happily. If he'd noticed the silent Anglo-Saxon, he showed no sign of minding.

The woman looked me over. "You're interviewing?"

"Yes."

"Well, I hope to *god* they hire you!" she exploded. "We could use the extra body!"

5

"THEY" TURNED OUT to be two entire floors of a Los Angeles skyscraper—a hundred attorneys and their "support staff"—which everyone referred to as "the California office."

Back in law school, I'd heard my fellow students complain about day-long, out-of-town interviews. I'd listened with a sense of smug superiority: I'd known from my first day that I would work for Julian Warneke. Julian had defended my parents when they'd broken into a military installation to swat missile nose cones with a ball-peen hammer; and when they'd blocked the entrance to Dow Chemical to protest its production of napalm; and when they'd defied restraining orders on picket lines of unions they didn't even belong to. Julian had defended my parents—or rather, had put on a political show on their behalf—so often that he'd become sort of an honorary uncle.

All through law school, as I'd watched students don itchy suits and fret over their résumés, I'd felt relief and even (I must admit) mild contempt. And now it was my turn to smile all day like a beauty contestant; to field pompous questions designed to make me look stupid (as anything about Articles 7 and 9 of the Uniform Commercial Code will do); to explain why I'd graduated from law school at the advanced age of thirty-three (without mentioning the years I'd gypsyed around in love beads and moccasins); and basically, to bootlick for a chance at big bucks.

I felt like I'd walked onto the set of *Invasion of the Body-Snatchers*—and become a pod-grown Republican.

At the end of the day, I was treated to dinner at an ersatz Roman temple called the L.A. Athletic Club. Accompanying me were four men and one woman. Two of the men looked like Bob LeVoq, only more so. They boasted that the attorneys' lounge had two cross-country ski machines (Parris, Black downstairs had only one). The two older partners looked more like real-life (as opposed to daytime TV) lawyers. One of them, a middle-aged man in a red vest, told me a little about the San Francisco office as the others conferred passionately over the wine list.

"The majority of San Francisco's work comes from California Bank and Trust. The office bills them, oh, one and a half, two million a year. The bank complains, but they know we're worth it." He glanced at Milward somebody-or-other, the oldest partner at the table.

Milward sipped his water (iced, with a slice of lemon) and smiled primly.

The woman seated to my left, loosely tucked into an acre of raw silk (from what I could see, the wool industry would go broke relying on L.A. women), licked a bit of salt off her margarita glass. "I hear CBT just sent a RICO case to Millet, Wray and Weissel."

Jonathan red-vest looked annoyed. "We don't handle *all* their matters—but we do get *most* of them. Hannah

Crosby sent over a multimillion-dollar collection case yesterday. So I think one can assume"—there was a sarcastic edge to his voice—"that the bank is happy with Bob's work!"

The woman studied her menu. "*Hannah* is certainly happy with Bob's . . . 'work.' "

One of the lounge skiers snickered.

Jonathan weighed his butter knife as if tempted to fling it. "Bob's a *rainmaker*! We need a rainmaker in that office!" He glanced at me. "We like our San Francisco people to focus on client development! You'll be expected to actively court clients—you know, bar functions, client seminars, business lunches, things like that."

"Oh, of course," I enthused, loathing the idea. And then, because everyone continued looking at me, I felt compelled to feign further interest. "Is Mr. LeVoq the only partner in the San Francisco office?"

For a moment, no one answered. The silk-suited woman stared at Milward with undisguised curiosity.

And Milward, the apparent tribal elder, replied, "Other than Bill Mott? For now—yes!" He looked around the table, quelling challenge. The skier and the woman exchanged speaking looks. Milward went quietly back to perusing his menu.

Nodding with satisfaction, Jonathan continued. "There are some very good people up in S.F. Bob's from Boalt; Melinda's from Georgetown; Aasgar's a local boy—UCLA; and the two new people."

"Harvard and Columbia," the woman supplied.

Milward inquired, without looking at me, "You went where?"

"Malhousie." And at lightning speed, I added, "Top five. Stanford undergrad."

6

WITH THE JOB came a fifteen-by-twenty office, four leather chairs, two oak desks, some potted palms, and a natty secretary named Andrew McNee. McNee was a muscular fifty-five-year-old with a crew cut, a clipped mustache, and an irritable expression. He stepped into my taupe-and-peach office unannounced, and found me fondly petting my leather chair.

"Welcome to Wailes, Roth, Ms. Jansson."

"Call me Willa."

"I prefer to be called Mr. McNee."

I guessed he'd object to keeping his head lower than mine, too. "All right."

"I should mention that I'm gay," he added, with crabby dignity.

As I'd had no intention of falling in love with him, I took the news well. "All right," I said again.

"I don't like my associates to think that I'm trying to hide it." He looked like a rich country squire in his

17

tweed suit, plain wool vest, and brogues. In fact, he
was too well dressed to be a heterosexual: men don't
bother looking that good for women.

"Oh, um, thank you. Do you know—is there a coffee
machine around here?" After two months of unemployment, it had been torture, getting up at seven. If I
didn't get some coffee soon, I'd slide off my chair.

McNee pointed to my telephone, which resembled a
space shuttle control panel. "Buzz Rhonda. She'll bring
you any potable or comestible you desire."

Rhonda was McNee's secretary. McNee, I gathered,
did all the document production and correspondence,
and Rhonda did the Xeroxing and filing. (She probably
called McNee "sir.")

I wondered what Mother would think of my secretary
(once removed) fetching my coffee. Mother was a great
one for preserving employee dignity. At restaurants, she
always tried to bus her own table. "I can get my own
coffee if—"

"Buzz Rhonda," McNee repeated, ending the matter.

A law firm with room service. I could live with it.

I was pouring coffee out of my third thermos carafe
of the day and painstakingly reading some loan documents when a balding man with perfect posture brought
me an armload of case files. "Nineteen receivables
cases," he said smugly. "Basically a full caseload."
Colin Aasgar was the third most senior attorney in the
office, after Bob and Melinda. "Take a look at them
tonight and we'll discuss them in the morning."

It was seven-thirty P.M. I already had my jacket on.
I was starving, and more urgently, I needed a joint. I
considered telling Aasgar that I already had a full case-
load, thanks to Bob and Melinda. But I could see
Aasgar already knew; his smile would have shamed a
B-movie Nazi. "Shouldn't take but a few hours to look

through them," he drawled. "Come to my office at around seven."

He hovered a moment, apparently waiting for me to say something I'd regret later. I slipped off my suit jacket.

For the next three hours, I read the tiny print whereby banks wrap their tentacles around debtors' assets. I read bankruptcy notices. I read Complaints by unsecured creditors, claiming they'd be ruined if the bank foreclosed on their supplier/distributor/client's assets; Complaints by debtors, claiming the bank had engineered their bankruptcies by "tortious business interference and premeditated under-collateralization"; and Complaints by debtors' employees, claiming the company had filed bankruptcy for the sole purpose of thwarting the union. Everybody wanted millions in bad faith damages from the bank. The bank merely wanted everything the debtors owned.

For ninety thousand a year, I'd do anything but break the debtors' thumbs.

7

IT WAS AFTER midnight by the time I dragged myself up my apartment building stairs. When I got to the first-floor landing, my landlord popped his head out the door, yawning extravagantly. He opened the door wider to reveal an African shirt stretched tight across his belly, corduroy pants that were unhemmed and threadbare, crooked-toed bare feet, and lank gray hair that hung untidily around his shoulders. "Earth woman!" He yawned again, his septuagenarian skin the color of raw fish. "Come in a second."

I walked into Ben Bubniak's apartment. The walls were lined with pulp art posters of science fiction book covers—five-headed beasts skewered by naked warriors, evil she-giants with spiked metal bras, globe-headed space priests with glowing eyes—and there were stacks of sci-fi books in every dusty corner. A computer and its family of peripherals nested on a library table. Here and there, wedged between crates of pamphlets, were unmatched pieces of inherited furniture. I sat carefully on a couch edged with knobby wooden roses and filled (apparently) with brick dust; built for Torquemada's waiting room, perhaps. It certainly hadn't been cleaned since then.

Still yawning, Ben said, "I was talking to your mother." He sat opposite me, on a love seat with springs capable of vasectomizing the unwary guest.

Beside him was a wooden crate full of pamphlets from Ben's desktop publisher: the conspiracies of the Trilateral Commission; the secret landing of the New Jerusalem in the Mojave Desert; proof that George Bush is the Beast whose number is the number of a man.

"Do you have any pot?" I wasn't up to discussing my mother straight.

Ben reached under the love seat for his pot tin. "We were talking about that homicide lieutenant." He opened the tin and pawed through an assortment of baggies, pulling a tightly rolled joint from one of them. "Did you know his family's filthy rich?"

"So he's a good catch?" The look on Ben's face told me that wasn't what he meant. "Hurry up and light that thing!"

"They own Italo–American Bank," he continued disapprovingly.

"Light the joint!"

He blinked at me, surprised at my tone. I snatched it away and lit it myself.

"Italo–American is the bank that evicted all those seniors from Hotel—"

"I don't care!" I exhaled too soon, searing my throat with uncooled smoke. "I don't care if the Surgelatos own Soweto! The lieutenant killed someone who came an inch away from killing *me*! And you guys act like it's the blackest moment since the execution of the Rosenbergs."

Ben shook his head sadly, muttering, "Earth woman!" He shifted sideways and reached into a fruit crate beside his chair. From it, he extracted a piece of paper, printed on both sides and folded in thirds.

I squinted at the pamphlet's caption. *"Don't* tell me you think he's in league with the Trilateral Commission!"

"I think your attitude is exactly what the commission is trying to foster, on a global scale."

"What attitude?"

"Like it says—here, take it!—the commission is trying to sap our moral outrage over violations of individual rights! Willa, don't you see? They chortle with glee when people like you lose their commitment—"

"Commitment to what? What should I be committed to that makes it okay for someone to try to murder me?" I stood up, joint trembling in my hand. "I'm sick of Mother's bullshit!"

Ben's expression grew stern; with his watery blue eyes, hoary hair, and wrinkled testament of a face, he could look quite impressively stern. "Maybe it's your own bullshit you're sick of!"

I ran upstairs, to get wasted in peace.

8

UNFORTUNATELY, MY FATHER was lying on my futon couch, a pile of books balanced on his belly. They fluttered with bookmarks as he transferred them to my coffee table. I could tell from the jackets that we were in for a rough session: Karl Marx, Eugene Debs, Michael Harrington, Sweezy & Baron, Martin Luther King, and even, god help me, Henry David Thoreau.

"No!" I said emphatically. "You are not going to quote *Walden* and *Das Kapital* to me! I'm going to represent banks! I'm going to open a charge account! I'm going to buy a decent couch! And the world is not going to go to hell because of it—just like it's not going to improve because of Mother's halfway house!"

My mother had inherited a house in the posh Marina district, and she'd turned it into a boarding house for paroled felons; a "fresh-start commune," she called it. The requirements for admission seemed to be a heinous, unrepented crime and an assortment of facial tics. A demonic expression was a plus. (Needless to say, the neighbors were frantically circulating petitions and complaining to friends in high places.)

My father stacked his books neatly. He had the look of a parent discovering contraceptives in his teenager's sock drawer.

"I'm thirty-five years old!" I erupted. "I've been to a million marches. I've spent two months in jail. I've proofread fifty thousand radical pamphlets. I've worked in a left-wing labor firm, and—"

"What good did it all do?" My father sat forward on the futon, nearly spilling off as the soft edge collapsed. "Willa! You can't measure accomplishment by externals!" He opened a dog-eared paperback, clearing his throat to read aloud.

"Don't! I don't care what Martin Luther King has to say about it! I *don't* have a dream! I don't care what we've accomplished on the ethereal plane!" I groped behind me, for the ashtray on my bookcase. "Look around! Ronald Reagan is president! Marijuana's still illegal! The Domino Theory has risen from the grave!" I stubbed out Ben's roach, concluding, "The left wing can finish self-destructing without me! I just want—"

"A new couch?" My father made it sound like the most ignoble of all possible desires.

"Exactly." I considered mentioning I wanted a television too, but decided he'd had enough of a shock.

"And you don't care what you have to do to get it." When had his pale hair turned white?

"Daddy, believe me—Wailes, Roth is politically neutral! They sue huge corporations for defaulting on loans! It's like suing Godzilla on behalf of Megalon! It's a wash, political karma-wise. It doesn't—"

"It doesn't solve the problem, Willa!"

"*Nothing* solves the problem, Daddy!"

He slumped deeper into the futon. "Do you hear yourself? Do you hear the lies you're letting yourself—"

"Lies? Me? You guys are so knee-jerk you wouldn't know the truth if it—if it—"

"Foreclosed on our mortgage?"

9

AT SEVEN THE next morning, when I knocked on Colin Aasgar's office door, I was still a little high. Maybe stoned is a better word—there was nothing elevated about the way I felt. I'd stayed up until two smoking pot and ignoring the pile of books my father had left behind. I felt, and probably looked, like the walking dead, but I was on time, and I was prepared.

Aasgar, however, was not there. Aasgar did not saunter into work until nine-thirty. No one at Warneke's firm would have summoned me hours early; I felt a stab of homesickness for my former coworkers and my dingy old office.

I found Aasgar closeted with Bob LeVoq. The two men were laughing, boxing up case files.

I told Aasgar that several of the cases he'd given me required immediate attention because statutes of limitations were about to run. I tried to keep the reproach out of my voice; some of the cases were two years old, and Aasgar had done nothing with them in all that time.

"Go to it, then," he said carelessly. Imagine bothering him with trifles like impending malpractice.

Then—to my very great surprise—Bob LeVoq countermanded the order. "Do the Cal Bank and Trust cases first!"

"But there's no statute of limitations problem with those. It's the Mercantile—"

"Do CBT first."

"But the S/L will run on Mercantile's—"

"CBT," LeVoq repeated, with a sly wink at Aasgar.

As I walked by Melinda's open door, she looked up and motioned to me. I entered an office lined with oak-framed diplomas and certificates. They were matted in mauve to match her carpet. "Did Aasgar give you some work?"

"Nineteen cases." I told her about the statute of limitations problem. "There's no way I can do California Bank and Trust's work first and still file Mercantile's claims on time. I need help." I added petulantly, "Colin doesn't seem that busy—he's just sitting around with Bob boxing up files."

I expected Melinda to be annoyed with Colin and Bob. I certainly was.

Instead, she seemed to go into shock. Her skin grew very pale, her freckles standing out like splotched ink. She just sat there, staring through me. Finally she mumbled, "The slimy bastard."

I'd never seen anyone take a statute of limitations so hard.

I waited for her to tell me what to do. She swiveled her antique oak chair toward the window, and looked down at the financial district traffic. Finally, one of her long-fingered hands walked itself to the telephone and punched a few buttons. Into her speaker, she said, "Get me Bill Mott."

While Mott was being gotten, I stepped back into Melinda's line of vision. "What should I do about Mercantile?"

"What? Oh, do their work, of course. Forget what Bob said. Bob's not important anymore."

A voice crackled in her phone speaker. "I have Mr. Mott for you."

Melinda rested her fingertip on the "speak" button. She seemed to be waiting for me to leave.

On my way out, I heard her moan, "Bob and Colin *are* leaving—and they think they're taking CBT!"

10

I WAS READING a book titled *Obtaining A Writ of Attachment*. It wasn't *Gone With the Wind*, but I had a million dollars worth of assets to attach before dinner. I found it mildly entertaining—it was the first time I'd ever posed a threat to a Jaguar-Mercedes dealership. I said with satisfaction, "Take that, capitalist running dog!"

From my doorway, a cough.

I looked up to find Melinda Karastatos standing there. "I don't mean to interrupt the revolution, but we have a lunch date with Hannah Crosby." Speaking the name aloud made her shoulders climb. "The Northern California Vice President of California Bank and Trust."

Obtaining A Writ of Attachment was not a difficult book to put down.

On our way out, Andrew McNee stopped me to say, "You have a call coming in, Ms. Jansson."

Melinda clutched my arm and pulled me past McNee's desk (a mere acre of mahogany in the park-sized outer office). She called over her shoulder, "Take a message, please."

McNee nodded with mild exasperation, as if there were no end to the things demanded of him. As we passed the tree-sized flower arrangement on the receptionist's marble counter, I heard McNee repeat a name into the telephone. "Bud Hopper. Yes, I'll ask her to return your call. Thank you," he said crisply.

The mystery Republican. I shook free of Melinda's grasp a second too late. McNee had already hung up. And Melinda said, "Believe me, it's not a good idea to keep Hannah waiting!"

We were soon part of the crush of humanity spewing from financial district towers. Maîtres d' appeared like elegant barkers in restaurant doorways, and food smells mingled with the cold bay breeze. I was jostled by English wool suits and trod upon by Italian leather shoes. I caught wisps of conversation about the Talking Heads and the new nanny and the tanning room at the Bay Club, and I was peripherally aware of gridlocked traffic, designer clothes in store windows (I could afford them now!), and alabaster bank facades. Melinda informed me that Hannah Crosby was "the original WASP princess-cum-bitch-goddess."

Then abruptly, she tugged me into a restaurant.

I looked at the pale pink tablecloths and exotic flower arrangements. And realized where I was.

I planted my feet, trying to pull away. Melinda looked irritated. Also distracted. She stepped farther inside with a shrug, expecting me to follow.

And I had to, of course. I followed her to an ornately carved podium where a ball-gowned woman guarded the reservation book. The book was fuchsia leather, emblazoned with silver script that read *René's*.

The woman conferred briefly with Melinda, then consigned us to a stiff-spined maître d'. He zigzagged through a constellation of tiny tables, apparently indifferent whether we followed. All around us, tuxedoed waiters deboned mesquite-grilled trout and offered corks for sniffing. None of them looked familiar, except in their determinedly handsome gayness.

None of them knew or cared that I'd returned to the scene of Julian Warneke's murder.

It had been less than five months since my former boss, true to habit, had eaten the garnish on his dessert plate—and discovered the hard way that it was poison hemlock.

I stopped at a table where six businessmen slumped over prime rib. We'd been sitting at that table, Julian and I and his three law partners. Enjoying a five-hundred-dollar lunch while discussing the labor problems of cannery workers.

Now, one of the businessmen cast an ogling glance at me, and I moved hastily away, catching up with Melinda and the maître d'. A few tables away, a bosomy woman in a gray silk blouse motioned to Melinda. She had high cheekbones, big black eyes, and a delicate nose, all heavily troweled with makeup. When she bent to put her briefcase on the floor, I saw that her black hair, secured with a pearl clip, was nearly waist length.

Melinda waved back, muttering through smiling lips, "Slut!"

It was going to be a fun lunch, all right.

Over Evian Water and salmon soufflé, I learned that Hannah Crosby had risen through the ranks of California Bank and Trust's legal department. For the last three years, she'd been Northern California Vice President in charge of legal affairs. Because of the volume of CBT's legal work, Hannah farmed most of it out to our firm. "I keep a semi-supervisory eye on things, of course," she informed me.

Whatever Melinda might think of her, Hannah Crosby clearly liked herself very much. It was apparent in the supercilious lift of her brows when she spoke to the waiter, in her superior drawl when she discussed her job, and in her out-of-the-blue, disparaging reference to Bob LeVoq's wife as "a *housewife*, in *this* day and age."

Melinda spent the better part of half an hour letting Hannah Crosby tell me about herself. Melinda interrupted only to ask questions designed to make Hannah feel important.

So I was surprised when, over coffee, Melinda said a trifle too innocently, "I understand William Mott is meeting with Pablo Villa-Fuentes this evening."

"Oh?" Hannah Crosby pressed a sliver of orange rind to the lip of her demitasse. (To cut the acidity of the coffee, a waiter explained; macha me—I tossed mine back, acid and all.)

"Yes," Melinda continued nonchalantly. "I believe they're going to the symphony."

Hannah sipped daintily, regarding Melinda over the rim of her cup. A slight frown creased her forehead.

Melinda smiled. "Bill was a Rhodes scholar, you know. He spent his research year in Spain—his Spanish is quite fluent. Castilian.'' She turned to me. ''Pablo Villa-Fuentes is the president of CBT. He's a very charming man.'' A cold light shone in her eyes. ''You'll meet him at the retreat.''

I had no idea what the ''retreat'' might be; I envisioned scrambling downhill through volleys of cannon fire. But I murmured, ''Great!''

Melinda turned back to Hannah. ''Bob won't be at the retreat this year. Bill thought it would be better to send me and Willa instead.''

Hannah's eyes grew round. She clunked her cup into its saucer. A sliver of glazed porcelain bounced onto the tablecloth. ''I thought the retreat was for clients and *partners* only.''

''I'm up for partnership at the next shareholders' meeting.'' She smiled, blushing slightly.

Hannah smiled back. The effort almost cracked her makeup. ''And Willa? Surely *she* . . . ?''

Melinda addressed her reply to me, a hint of amusement in her tone. ''A new client specifically asked that Willa attend.''

I shook my head. ''I don't think I know any of your—''

''His name is Bud Hopper. He just left public service—Department of the Interior, I think—to go back into the family business. Apparently Hopper read some article you wrote, and now he wants to meet you.''

''I didn't think anybody read student law review articles.'' Especially not Republican bureaucrats. Especially not articles proposing unrestricted immigration coupled with a national full-employment policy and mandatory unionism.

Melinda shrugged. ''That's what I heard. Anyway, it's an honor to be invited.''

I had a sudden, sick flash of paranoia. It couldn't be the article; law review articles did not generate fans. It had to be the murders. My name had made the national

news twice in connection with multiple murders. Bud
Hopper (whoever the hell he was) must have heard my
name linked to the murders—and taken it upon himself
to get me hired by Wailes, Roth. Now he'd gotten me
invited to the firm's partner/client retreat. *Why?*

"Who *is* Bud Hopper, anyway?"

"I don't know. You'll find out at the retreat." Melinda wasn't interested in Bud Hopper. She was watching Hannah.

Hannah Crosby scowled at her linen napkin, folding
it into a tight, tiny square. Her fingers worked stiffly
and furiously.

And Melinda, with crocodile tears in her voice, said,
"What a pity Bob won't be there!"

11

B OB LE VOQ VANISHED. He didn't come into the office
for days on end—days, it happened, that William Mott
was in San Francisco, conferring with Melinda Karastatos. My secretary, Mr. McNee, confided, in a rare fit
of garrulousness, that Bob's absence was having little

impact on office routine; Bob rarely generated work for his secretary, and he usually sent associates to court to argue his motions.

Bud Hopper (whoever he might be) also vanished. When I tried the Washington, D.C., phone number he'd left with McNee, I was told he'd gone to South Africa on business. (I hoped my parents didn't learn I owed my job to an apartheid supporter.)

In the meantime, I was buried alive in work. I barely had time to pack for the partner/client retreat, which was being held at a luxurious "Wilderness Conference Center" near Yosemite. The partners, it seemed, had tired of Pebble Beach and Cabo San Lucas. They'd decided to "do" the Mariposa Estates Hotel.

I'd heard of the Mariposa, and knew I should be impressed by it. My room, one of their cheapest, was costing the firm $174 a night. It had oiled pine walls, Early American reproduction furniture, and Navajo print rugs, bedspread and curtains. Senior partners and clients had mahogany-paneled penthouse suites with intricately carved hearths, fully stocked bars and grandiose forest views. My ground-floor room looked out on a walkway bustling with linen-laden maids. Beyond that were the wilderness tennis courts.

The dining and conference rooms were equally impressive—Versailles redone in Native American. Vast halls were hung with Hopi weavings. Cathedral alcoves displayed Iroquois baskets filled with Mariposa Wilderness Experience matchbooks. From every window, spectacular mountain views made me feel guilty about not wanting to simplify, simplify. But even if I'd wanted to commune with nature, I couldn't have. I'd brought along a briefcase full of work.

Melinda urged me to set the work aside. "You've only got three more years until your partnership vote! It'll take you that long to get to know everybody! Consider your prospects. Do some networking!"

"A malpractice claim by Mercantile won't do my prospects any good. I'll network at dinner."

At dinner I discovered that I was not going to meet the mysterious Bud Hopper, after all. I was sitting with some Los Angeles partners—muscle-bound lounge skier Sean Kowalski; Jonathan Seeder, who'd defended LeVoq as a rainmaker; Bill Mott, looking like Macchiavelli in black tie; and Milward Kael, Bill's virtual twin in Republican pruniness. Also at the table were Hannah Crosby, Melinda Karastatos, and a man from Coast Factors (whatever a factor might be). Melinda whispered excitedly that we were sitting with three of the California office's most important partners: Mott, Kael and Seeder. As a result, I sat so straight my spine ached. I was the only woman in the immense dining room in a business suit. The only one who was not showing some breast or shoulder. The only one whose hair was not moussed to defy gravity. Some wilderness experience. I smiled so fixedly, my cheeks were close to spasm. I wanted to sneak outside and smoke a joint.

At least it had been comfortable, working for Julian Warneke. I'd known him most of my life. And he hadn't paid me enough to make me smile when I didn't want to.

When you sell your soul, your cheek muscles are part of the bargain, I guess.

Beside me, William Mott sipped mineral water and inclined his head toward Hannah Crosby. She sat very straight in a bare-shouldered eruption of ruffles. She was complaining that the bill for some case or other had seemed "rather inflated." Her unperturbed smile didn't fool anyone, and wasn't meant to.

On the other side of me, Melinda Karastatos stiffened. With a silencing gesture in Melinda's direction, Mott told Hannah, "I discussed the matter with Pablo last week. The bill is rather large—Bob's billing rate far exceeds that of our associates, and I believe you particularly wanted Bob to work on the case? I did offer to effect a small good-will adjustment. But Pablo recognizes the importance of not cutting corners where a multimillion-dollar judgment is involved.''

Crosby's smile grew pinched. ''The case is within my purview. Pablo doesn't understand the issues as well as I do.''

''Actually''—Mott squeezed a lime wedge over his Perrier—''we discussed it in some detail.''

Hannah Crosby buttered her bread as if she were stropping a razor.

Sean Kowalski began discussing a white-water kayaking trip he was organizing. He particularly wanted me to go, it seemed. I smiled noncommittally. My idea of an outdoor adventure is waiting for the streetcar.

I was drinking gin rickeys (I'd heard that, in quantity, they're a little like weak mescaline). By the time the waiters served the soup, I'd imbibed a fair amount of liquid courage. Enough to ask Bill Mott, ''Is Bud Hopper here?''

Mott had replaced his half glasses with full glasses. His magnified eyes made him look supernaturally intelligent. ''I understand he can't make it, after all.''

''Do you know him very well?''

''Hopper? No. I know *of* him. I've never met him myself.''

''You've only talked to him on the phone?''

Mott blinked at me. I could hear Melinda determinedly ask John Seeder about his children's youth soccer team. Mott said, ''Not personally. I understand that you knew him rather well.''

I shook my head. ''I'd never heard the name before your firm contacted me.''

Kowalski interrupted to ask Mott about his golf game.

But Milward Kael, looking stooped and dyspeptic, brought us back to Hopper. From across the table, he murmured, ''I understand Mr. Hopper put in a good word for you with the New York office.'' His voice was quiet, and his lips hardly moved. But suddenly, all around the table, voices were lowered so as not to drown him out.

"So I was told.''

Mott addressed Kael. "He requested that Willa attend the retreat, also.''

Kael raised his brows. "It's a pity he couldn't make it, then.''

"I don't know him,'' I repeated. "I'm a little surprised at the interest he's taken—''

Kael looked so astonished that I stopped talking. One by one, everyone on his side of the table stopped talking. Hannah Crosby smiled.

I turned around to find Bob LeVoq threading his way across the room, slapping clients' backs, pausing to greet partners, laughing with his head thrown back.

I glanced at Bill Mott. He watched LeVoq with cool appraisal. I wouldn't have wanted him looking at me that way.

Melinda scowled at her salad plate.

Bob slipped into an empty chair at a table halfway across the room. Most of the people at that table looked smug and well groomed: lawyers and bank officers. There were also a couple of executives from Excelsior Motion Pictures. I'd asked Melinda about them because they looked like movie stars. Bob chatted with an Excelsior woman in plunging décolletage. He looked as relaxed and happy as ever, talking to the woman's breasts and looking around in a who's-at-the-party kind of way. When he spotted us, he smiled and waved, then turned jovially back to the Excelsior neckline.

An army of waiters created a diversion by clearing away the soup and salad plates. William Mott answered Sean Kowalski's question about his golf game, as if he'd just that moment been asked. Jonathan Seeder sipped his wine and watched Melinda, his lips curling with malignant satisfaction. Melinda, taking her cue from Mott, began telling Seeder all about a Judges' Night dinner she'd attended. Hannah Crosby began flirting with the man from Coast Factors, laughing loudly at whatever he said—to his apparent surprise. Milward Kael stared at Bob LeVoq's back as if measuring him for voodoo pins.

As the waiters turned our coffee cups right side up, I noticed Bob LeVoq hurrying out of the dining room.

For the next forty-five minutes, we endured joke-filled speeches of welcome from Jonathan Seeder and other L.A. partners, and joke-filled happy-to-be-here speeches from some of the bank clients, including Hannah Crosby's suavely foreign-looking boss, Pablo Villa-Fuentes. (Hannah Crosby was the only woman in the room who did not smile admiringly during his speech.) Finally, people stood up and began to regroup. Some drifted toward the piano bar, some hiked to the flagstone pool, spa, and miniwaterfall, and others staked out alcoves for a game called Pictionary. Melinda was bent over William Mott, making intense, jerky hand motions as she whispered to him. Then she noticed me sidling away and broke off the conversation, her hands wilting to her sides.

I dashed out of the room before she could cajole me into further networking. I retreated to my room to smoke a joint.

But when I unlocked my door, I found Bob LeVoq lying on my bed with his shirt off.

12

"**B**OB! I THINK this is my room."

LeVoq chuckled. "I know." He stood up and crossed the room, leaning past me to close the door I'd left open. He'd changed into gray cotton slacks and gray Topsiders without socks. He had a small waist and his hairless chest and arms showed evidence of a weight-lifting regimen. The pumped-up body didn't match the boyish face.

I was wondering if he was going to ask me to go home so he could have my room. He didn't. He wrapped his arms around me and began sucking on my lips.

I was pushing on his chest and *mmph*ing, disgusted to be touching bare flesh—anybody's bare flesh.

LeVoq was not discouraged. He began groping me in a way that reminded me of my one and only date with a Stanford frat boy.

I had no idea how I'd gotten into the situation, and I wasn't sure how to get out of it. I wasn't frightened, but the whole thing was damned inconvenient. Silly, too.

I managed to turn my face away and say, "Stop grabbing me! I'm going to scream if you don't—"

Arms still around me, he took a few steps and tipped his body backward. We fell onto the bed, me on top of him.

I resorted to cliché. I kneed him in the groin.

I scrambled to my feet and watched him curl into the usual kneed-in-the-groin position. "What are you doing in my room?"

He was trying to sit up, obviously at great pains not to grab himself and howl. "I thought—Hopper said—"

"*Bud* Hopper?" I looked down at him, ready to knee him again if he made any sudden moves. "Who the hell *is* Bud—"

"He said you had, well, a *thing* about—" He was very red of face, even his neck and chest were red. It occurred to me that he was blushing. "Well, a thing about, you know, *me*," he concluded with faint hope.

"What!" I considered kneeing him again, for the hell of it. "Haven't you ever heard of sexual harassment? You must be nuts! And who the *hell* is Bud Hopper, anyway? How's he supposed to know what I—"

"He said you liked—"

"Wait a minute. Did you talk to this man in person?"

"No, on the phone. We've been talking about D.C. He said he'd put in word for me at . . . Anyway, Mott and Spender vouched for him, so—"

"But you've never seen him?"

He shook his head.

"And you took the advice of someone you'd never met—a voice on the telephone—to attack a woman?"

LeVoq stood up, edging toward the door as he snatched a Lacoste shirt from the bedside chair. "Whoa, this is weird. Really. I thought—"

I put my body between LeVoq and the door. "Tell me exactly what Hopper said about me."

LeVoq's hair fell limply over his damp forehead. Pockmarks in his round cheeks remained pale under his general flush. He pulled the shirt over his head, mumbling, "Well, we were talking about—Washington. Girls in Washington. And he, um, he said he knew you pretty well. Said he'd talked to you about me, in fact." He seemed to wince. "Well, without getting too graphic, he said you, um, appreciated an aggressive approach."

I moved away from the door.

On his way out, LeVoq intentionally brushed against me, as if a last encounter with his muscles would change my mind.

I slammed the door behind him, fuming. How much of the story was true, and how much was an excuse for frat-boy behavior?

And *who*, who the *hell* was Bud Hopper?

13

FIRST THING THE next morning, I phoned the San Francisco police, Homicide detail. They told me Lieutenant Don Surgelato was not available. As far as I was concerned, he hadn't been available for two and a half months. "Is Inspector Krisbaum there?"

Daniel Krisbaum had been in charge of investigating the Julian Warneke homicide, and I'd gotten to know him slightly. He was an overweight and sloppy man, not particularly smart or particularly friendly. But he wasn't a stranger; my story would sound silly to a stranger.

"Krisbaum speaking." Even his voice was sloppy, not quite tenor and not quite baritone.

"This is Willa Jansson."

Silence.

"You remember me, don't you?"

"Certainly do! How are things?"

"Crappy!"

He snickered. "And how are *you* today, Danny?"

"Sorry, I thought you were really asking."

"Okay, I'm really asking. How are things?"

"I'm at the Mariposa Estates Conference Center at a lawyer/client retreat for my new job. From what I gather, my boss is planning to leave the firm and steal away the firm's biggest client, and some of the other partners have been plotting against him, and now he's shown up here even though he's not supposed to be, and last night he came to my room—" I stopped to take a breath. "This isn't making any sense, is it?"

"Are we talking about a crime? Did this boss of yours hurt you, or—"

"No, not yet. I mean, he's not going to hurt me ever, but see, he's not supposed to be here. There are all these *tensions* in the firm revolving around this man, and I was kind of worried that . . ." I was suddenly glad I hadn't troubled Surgelato with my nebulous foreboding.

"And you're thinking somebody's going to bump him off?" Krisbaum's sigh was exasperated, but not completely unsympathetic. "We see this kind of thing, every once in a while. Somebody's involved in a murder case, and the next time there's a family fight or whatever, it scares the bejesus out of them. They think somebody's going to get killed. The shrinks say sometimes the stress of a murder leaves residual paranoia—"

"No, I'm not just worrying because of Julian." I stopped, rubbing my eyes. Maybe Krisbaum was right. Maybe I'd been conditioned by my bad experiences to expect murder whenever I saw strong, negative emotions. "What worries me most is this Bud Hopper guy—" I gasped, startled by a knock on my door. "Can you hold on? Someone's at the door."

A man in a room service uniform handed me a sealed white envelope with my room number on it. I thanked him, found my handbag and tipped him three dollars. (Hell, I could afford it!)

When I got back on the line, I found that Krisbaum had switched me back to the receptionist because he'd had another call coming in. Could she take my number and have the inspector return my call?

I gave her the number taped to the hotel telephone. As she read it back to me, I opened the envelope. A glossy rectangle dropped into my lap.

"Wait a minute—don't hang up!" I interrupted.

I recognized the nature of the rectangle. I was looking at the back of a snapshot.

I turned it over. It had been taken from outside my hotel room window, from the path the maids and busboys used.

The photograph was blurry, shot from outside using only the light from the room's lamps. There were black streaks on either side, apparently two halves of an incompletely closed curtain. The picture was grainy and dim, but to someone who already knew what it was, there was no mistaking it. It was me and Bob LeVoq, sprawled across my bed.

"Listen," I said to the woman. "I've *got* to talk to Lieutenant Surgelato! It's very urgent!"

"I'm sorry, the lieutenant's not in his office. If you'd care to speak to one of the other—"

"Leave a message for him, *please*. Tell him to come right away to the Mariposa Conference Center. It's just north of Yosemite. I'm in the main hotel. Room one-fourteen. Tell him . . . Tell him Willa is in trouble. Please."

"That's W-i-l-l-a?" she asked calmly. "May I ask what this is in regard to, please?"

"I've already explained it to Inspector Krisbaum."

"All right, then. Thank you. Have a nice morning."

14

But it wasn't Don Surgelato who rapped on my door right after lunch. It was Danny Krisbaum.

He wore baggy gray slacks and he carried a wrinkled brown sport jacket. His cordovan belt dangled free of its loop. His striped tie gaudily transversed a salmon shirt. His jowly face was damp, and a few thin wisps of hair clung to what would soon be a bald dome.

I'd asked for Don, and I'd gotten Krisbaum. I turned my back on the Homicide Inspector (as they are so quaintly called, in San Francisco).

I wasn't my mother; I wasn't trying to cause Surgelato trouble. He might have called, at least. He might have feigned concern.

I heard Krisbaum step inside and close the door. He walked past me and dropped into a wide chair upholstered in a neo-Navajo print. "Hot drive," he commented.

I fished the snapshot out of my shirt pocket. "I got scared when I saw this. That's why I left the message."

I was embarrassed; did he wonder why I'd asked for Don?

Krisbaum matter-of-factly held out his hand.

I handed him the picture, then sat on the bed. There were loan documents and pleadings spread all over it. I'd used them as an excuse not to go down to lunch with Melinda, and again later to avoid kayaking with the persistent Sean Kowalski. I'd been staring at them all morning, but I'd been thinking about Bob LeVoq.

"The lády, I take it, is you?" Krisbaum squinted at the picture, then at my bed. "Taken right here?" He twisted around, looking out the window. "From outside. Where'd you get this?"

"Room service brought it. The man is my boss, Bob LeVoq. I was telling you about him."

"You said he attacked you." Krisbaum held up the picture. "Is this what you meant?"

"He said Bud Hopper suggested it." I ran my fingers through my hair, wishing room service would come with another carafe of coffee.

"Bud Hopper being?"

"Who the hell knows? Nobody I've talked to has ever seen him! He got me this job, and he asked the firm to bring me to the retreat. Then he advised my boss to come to my room and jump on me. And nobody's even met him! He's just a voice on the phone to these people!"

"Hold it. What exactly are we talking about here? Are we talking rape? Blackmail?"

"Neither. Why didn't the lieutenant come?"

Krisbaum was looking a little cranky. "Better question is why did *anybody* come? This place happens to be four hours southeast of our jurisdiction. Besides which—" He loosened his tie and unbuttoned his shirt collar. "It's not S.O.P. for the lieutenant to investigate cases. He's an administrator. What he did before, with the law school case and the Warneke case, that was

unusual. They were big cases, so he got involved,
maybe more than an administrator should. But ordi-
narily, it's us inspectors who do the legwork. That's *if*
we've got a homicide situation, which we do not appear
to have here." He looked around the room, confirming
the paucity of corpses. "So no offense, but you're lucky
anybody showed up."

"The lieutenant won't return my calls."

The inspector shrugged. "I'm not his engagement
secretary, Miss Jansson. I don't tell him who to call. I
got your message, and I came." He smiled weakly.
"And I'd feel a lot more welcome if you told room
service to bring me a cold beer."

I dialed room service, cringing when Krisbaum requested a Coors. "Joseph Coors provided secret aid
to the Contras, did you know that? He makes his employees take lie detector tests, and he busted their
union—"

"I'm drinking his beer, Miss Jansson, not marrying
his daughter. Oh, forget it. Cancel the beer. Just tell
me what's the problem."

I hung up the phone, and began telling Krisbaum
about Bud Hopper and the law review article that
couldn't possibly have impressed the Reagan administration (I hoped!); and about William Mott asserting
dominion over the San Francisco office; and Melinda's
hint that LeVoq was planning to leave and steal away
the firm's biggest client, whose vice president was apparently LeVoq's lover; and Mott currying favor with
LeVoq's lover's boss; and LeVoq showing up at the retreat when Mott told him he couldn't come; and then
showing up in my room because Bud Hopper told him
to. And who the hell *was* Bud Hopper, anyway?

Krisbaum had an "I-drove-all-the-way-out-here-for-
this?" expression on his face.

"Don't you see?" I squatted beside his chair. "There
is no Bud Hopper! It's just a name someone used to get

me this job, and get me to this retreat! And to get Bob LeVoq into my room!''

"Miss Jansson, do you want my honest opinion?''

"I'd rather have your dishonest sympathy! Look, California Bank and Trust is our biggest client; from what I gather, it keeps the San Francisco office solvent.''

"That may be the case, but—''

"It's one thing for Mott to power-struggle LeVoq into quitting. A lot of people would be happy about that. But it's a whole different ball game if LeVoq takes CBT with him!''

"All right, I see where you're going with this! But let's face it, when lawyers have business problems, they sue each other, they don't kill—''

"But suppose someone *did* want to kill Bob LeVoq. Look at the position I'm in. This would be the third murder case I've been involved in! Nobody would believe I didn't have something to do with it! Especially if the cops searched my room and found this!'' I snatched up the picture of me and Bob on the bed. "They'd think we were lovers!''

Krisbaum was rubbing the spot between his eyebrows (his third eye, my mother would have called it—assuming she thought cops had them). "Why did I cancel the beer?''

"Do you see what I mean?''

"Look, every business that's got more than one chief, you're going to get a power struggle situation. It's only human. But as far as big plots, and people getting killed—'' He shook his head. "Tell you the truth, I just don't see it. Not in the facts as you've presented them, anyway.''

"What about this Bud Hopper character? Why would someone tell LeVoq—''

"You're assuming LeVoq was telling you the truth. Maybe the guy was just weaseling out of a bad situation. You're a good-looking woman; maybe he just wanted to see how far you'd—''

''Even if there really is a Bud Hopper—''

''I can check that out.''

''—it doesn't mean somebody didn't use his name to get LeVoq into my room. Somebody wants to kill LeVoq and make it look like we were lovers.'' I scrutinized Krisbaum's face. ''Do you think? Maybe?''

''You know what it sounds like to me, Miss Jansson?''

''I'm afraid to ask.''

''Maybe, unconsciously, you *want* to be involved in another murder case.'' He stood slowly, pushing himself off the chair with both arms. The photograph fluttered to the floor. ''Maybe it's not my business to say so, but I'm getting the definite feeling you've got, well, some kind of a *thing* for the lieutenant.''

I bent down and retrieved the snapshot, mostly to avoid facing him. I did *not* want to be involved in another murder case—however true it might be that I had a ''thing'' for the lieutenant. I waved the photo in his face. ''How do you explain this?''

''You say LeVoq has a lover here?''

''Yes. She's second in command of the bank that's our biggest client.''

''Then ten'll get you twenty the picture makes its way to her. What you've got here, I think, is somebody trying to bust up a relationship. Somebody trying to make your boss look like a sleaze-ball.''

''He is a sleaze-ball.''

''So it was easy to set him up. Somebody that knew him pretty well, they could suggest he come to your room and give you a tumble. They could stand right out there''—he pointed to the window—''and take a couple of pictures. Get his girlfriend mad enough and the work problem solves itself, right? He's out of the firm, and she doesn't go with him. No need to kill anybody.''

I wasn't sure whether to feel relieved or angry. I *was* sure women my age shouldn't blush.

"Now you have to drive all the way back to San Francisco."

"I'll spend the night in Merced, I guess." He didn't seem to relish the thought. I've been to Merced; no one would relish the thought.

"It was nice of you to come."

He shrugged.

I walked him through the lobby and on my way back, I stopped at the desk to complain that I'd ordered coffee and it still hadn't arrived. When I turned around, I noticed a man rising from a chair. He was partially obscured by an island of dried flowers separating the walk-through area from an area of chairs and couches.

I stopped. I'd have recognized him in a tunnel in the dead of night.

Five foot nine, too much muscle stuffed into too little suit, black hair brushed stiffly off a low forehead, thick brows hooding deep-set eyes, a crooked nose, a dimpled chin.

He stepped sideways, around the flower arrangement. He just stood there, twenty feet away from me.

He'd come, after all.

15

I closed the hotel room door behind us. What the hell was I supposed to say? After hearing Krisbaum's opinion, I thought my paranoia was a little neurotic.

And I had to say something. This was not going to be a take-me-in-your-arms-you-fool kind of meeting. I'd known that as soon as Lieutenant Don Surgelato said, "I got your message, Miss Jansson." (And his eyes said, This had better be important!)

He didn't sit down. He continued standing near the door. His suit was rumpled. A four-hour drive, Krisbaum had said. Surgelato was thinner than I remembered. There seemed to be more suit fabric available for wrinkling.

It was easier to look at his suit than his face.

He said, "Danny was here. I waited until he left."

"He got my message too." I glanced at him. Ouch. Glanced away. He didn't approve of me routing inspectors away from the Homicide detail.

"So what's the trouble?"

I wasn't exactly sure, anymore.

He turned away. Paced to the far end of the room. Ran a hand over his hair as he looked out the window.

He said, "What do you want? Another favor?"

My mother didn't appreciate what he'd done for her. And his career was in shambles.

He turned to face me, silhouetted against the bright afternoon light. "You certainly landed on your feet, didn't you? You must be making big money, now."

"Ninety thousand."

"Jesus Christ!"

He was just old enough (forty-five?) and just enough of a jock (a former quarterback for some team or other) for it to matter to him that a woman earned more money than he did.

I'd been thinking it was my mother and the whole Warneke murder thing, keeping us apart; but really, it was more than that.

I glanced at my nightstand. There was a quarter ounce of pot tucked under the Gideon Bible. Would he understand that I needed the stuff, illegal or not?

"I was afraid you'd be sorry," I said.

"Sorry! Sorry doesn't even—" He was frowning so deeply his eyes were lost in shadow. "It's not the political storm. You learn to weather those. It's what I did." More quietly. "Why I did it."

Krisbaum had told me at the time it was the lieutenant's "first shoot."

"Don—Lieutenant. I almost got killed. It's hard for me to get sentimental—"

"Sentimental! Is that what you think? I blew away a poor little murderer, and now I feel bad?" Anger made his olive skin unnaturally pale. "I'm a cop. I'm supposed to preserve evidence and stop crime. That poor little murderer's testimony might have netted us an underground organization, you realize that?" He looked like a man who'd turned down the Colonel's secret chicken recipe. "Christ! Who knows what we might have shaken out of the carpet if we'd have had a chance to question—" He stopped. Maybe he knew he was kidding himself. Warneke's killer wouldn't have told the police a goddam thing. "I didn't come here to talk about this."

Maybe it wasn't macho for a cop to be sorry he'd shot someone. Better to regret the lost opportunity to beat information out of a suspect.

I was no expert on that kind of mentality. What the hell was I supposed to say?

I said, "Krisbaum made me feel like an idiot. We have kind of a situation in my law firm. And I guess I'm still jumpy. I thought—Krisbaum says I'm wrong. I don't see any point in bothering you with it, too." Jesus, I was going to cry. What a pair: macho cop, weepy blonde. I bit the inside of my cheek. Thought tough thoughts. Willed the tears right back down their ducts. "I'm sorry I made you come all this way."

He continued to scowl at me. "Danny was in here a long time."

I shrugged. "It's a long job, talking sense into me."

The scowl began to fade. "What exactly is the problem?"

The snapshot of LeVoq was beside him on the lamp table. I guess I glanced at it, because he looked down at the table top.

He picked up the picture. Studied it. Looked at the bed. Turned around and looked out the window. Looked at the picture again.

"Who's the guy?"

"My boss."

"What's the picture mean?"

"He attacked me." Surgelato made a furious fist, scowling as he advanced toward me. I wasn't sure if he was angry at me or LeVoq. I continued hurriedly, "I stopped him, but somebody took this picture in the meantime. We couldn't have been on the bed more than a minute.''

Surgelato halted a couple of feet away from me. ''Why?''

''Krisbaum thinks somebody put LeVoq—Bob LeVoq, my boss—up to it. He thinks somebody took the picture to show it to LeVoq's girlfriend. His girl-friend is one of the firm's biggest clients. The firm's trying to get rid of LeVoq, I think—and still keep the client.''

''How'd you get the picture?''

''Room service.''

He shook his head. ''Krisbaum's off base. Why give *you* the picture?''

''I think—or I thought, anyway—that somebody wanted to kill LeVoq and make it look like I was his lover.''

''Why?''

''To frame me.''

''No, I mean, why did you think so?''

I sighed, backing up to the bed and sitting wearily on the edge. Loan documents were still spread over it. I could almost hear statutes of limitations expiring.

It was a long story. I hadn't eaten yet and I was dying for coffee. I was lovesick.

''I went through it all with Krisbaum. He convinced me—''

''Go through it again.''

I felt myself bristle. He'd interrogated me too many times in the last few years.

''No! I think Krisbaum's right. I've been stupid. There are all these job tensions! I confused them for something worse than they are. I've been seeing murder plots where there aren't any! Thank god!'' There was a knock at my door. If it wasn't my coffee, I'd scream. I walked to the door, saying, ''I was being paranoid! Krisbaum made me see that!''

My eyes were fixed at waist level as the door swung open. At first I blinked at the trim waist and flat belly in gray wool slacks. Where the hell was the coffee tray?

I looked up at Melinda Karastatos' face. She looked like a zombie, a buck-toothed, freckled zombie in an expensive pants suit. Her lips were a little blue.

She said, "Bob's dead."

I felt a rush of air as Surgelato crossed the room. Half my consciousness absorbed the news about Bob LeVoq; absorbed it without believing it.

The other half drunkenly rejoiced because Don Surgelato was touching me. He was standing beside me with his arm around me.

Melinda blinked at him, then looked at me again. "Bob's dead," she said. "Somebody killed Bob."

16

"IT'S BUD HOPPER!" I insisted. I was back to viewing Bud Hopper as the sinister architect of all my troubles. "He got me hired! He made them bring me to the retreat! He lied to Bob LeVoq about me!"

Surgelato was conferring with hotel security, waiting
for cops to come from Merced. I was standing in the
corner of a cherrywood and flagstone conference room
with Daniel Krisbaum. Krisbaum, it seemed, had a police radio in his car; he'd eavesdropped on Merced,
turning around when he heard the news about LeVoq.
He and Surgelato seemed embarrassed to see one another.

Krisbaum was frowning at Surgelato's back. Surgelato was bent over a conference table, one hand on the
waxed surface as the other made stabbing gestures at a
seated hotel security guard. The guard, a gawky youth
in a pressed khaki ranger uniform, looked up at the
lieutenant with respectful awe. Another "ranger" wrote
down everything Surgelato said.

I shook Krisbaum's arm. "You should be making sure
no one leaves the hotel!"

He favored me with a distracted glance. "Nobody's
leaving, don't worry."

"You should keep everyone in one room until the
Merced police get here!"

"This is not *Murder on the Orient Express*, Miss
Jansson. Trust me. We know what we're doing!"

"What if someone flees the jurisdiction?"

"You know your evidence code!"

"Flight can be used to infer guilt in a court of—Oh."

"Oh," he repeated.

"We're all lawyers. We all know that."

"Bingo."

"Are the Merced police going to question people in
here?"

"They're going to question people wherever they
want to."

"Are you and the lieutenant going to help them?"

"We're not the Hardy boys. There are rules about
where we do our jobs."

"How long do I have to stay here?"

"That's not up to me."

"And you absolutely can't give me the least hint—"

"No! No, I can't!" His voice rang with parental exasperation. It wasn't the first time I'd asked him for details about LeVoq's death. All I'd gotten so far was a terse yes to my question, "Is foul play suspected?"

I could hear commotion in the hall outside the conference room. Another Mariposa employee (his uniform suggesting the Native West department at Neiman-Marcus) stuck his head in and gestured to a guard. The guard loped over and conferred with him. A moment later, Surgelato left the ersatz rangers and joined us.

He took my arm, motioning with his head for Krisbaum to accompany us. "We've only got a few minutes before the Merced police get here."

As we crossed to the door, Krisbaum protested mildly, "Merced's gonna want to be the first to talk to everyone—including Miss Jansson."

To which Surgelato replied, "Gosh, Danny, you think the Merced police might get mad at me?"

Krisbaum chuckled.

His hand on the small of my back, Surgelato propelled me out of the hotel and along a well-swept stone walkway, past clusters of lawyers in Banana Republic hiking garb.

We walked under a leafy arbor to the back of the hotel. Surgelato hustled me through a field to a wooded spot beside a stream. It occurred to me that we couldn't be seen from the hotel.

It was late afternoon, too hot for someone in a corduroy skirt and long-sleeved shirt. The air smelled of dusty leaves, and tinkled with brook sounds. I sat on a fallen log, hoping the Mariposa had a dry-cleaning service.

Surgelato huddled briefly with Krisbaum, then squatted in front of me. A breeze ruffled his hair. "This morning something made you think Robert LeVoq was going to be murdered. That's why you phoned my office, isn't it?''

''Yes.''

''I want to know what made you think so.'' He squinted, though the sun was behind him. ''I want details. Everything you told Danny. More, if possible. As much as you can think of.''

''What happened to Bob?''

''No, you go first. Hindsight's going to creep into your story, anyway—it's inevitable. I want to try to minimize it.''

His request seemed reasonable, so I complied with it. I told him everything I'd told Krisbaum. Maybe a little more.

Surgelato listened more intently than Krisbaum had. He studied my face. (I wondered if two months of frustrated unemployment had aged me.)

Ultimately, I faltered to a stop.

Krisbaum cleared his throat and walked downstream, as if admiring the view.

Surgelato's face was two feet from mine. It was a rough, unintelligent face, but he was neither of those things. I wasn't exactly sure what he was.

He said, ''Robert LeVoq was poisoned.''

''Poisoned? How?''

He put his hands on my shoulders. He opened his mouth and shook his head as if the words just wouldn't come. And I knew without being told.

''Hemlock,'' I said. ''The same as Julian Warneke.''

17

Not quite the same as Julian Warneke. My former boss had been poisoned in dignified elegance at a French restaurant. Bob LeVoq was discovered on a marshy trailhead with a dirt-caked hemlock plant stuffed into his mouth.

I shrank from a plant that curled over my fallen log. I wouldn't know hemlock from hibiscus, but greenery in general seemed sinister. "Somebody *made* him eat it? Right out of the ground?"

"Maybe. Or maybe someone put it in his mouth after he was already dead. It took Warneke a few hours—well, never mind about Warneke. Hemlock *can* act quickly, but usually, it's a matter of hours. Or it could even be LeVoq ate it voluntarily, not knowing it was hemlock. We've seen a few cases of that. People thinking a plant is a psychotropic—"

"You think Bob ate hemlock by *mistake*? To get *high*?"

"I didn't say that. I just want to know if you think it's possible, from what you know of him."

"No! Even if LeVoq was hip enough to do drugs"— Surgelato seemed amused by my choice of adjective— "he'd have bought the finest processed chemicals. Cocaine, or some designer drug. I can't see him scarfing down weeds."

Krisbaum waddled back into view, looking like an upright bear. He bent painfully and picked up a few stones, skipping them over the water.

"The way LeVoq was found—his mouth could have been stuffed after he died," Surgelato mused. "But I'd say from the look of him he was definitely poisoned."

"Maybe he had a heart attack or something." I sounded like I was asking a favor.

Surgelato rose, offering a hand to help me up. "It didn't look that way to me, and I've seen quite a few—" He didn't have to say "dead bodies."

I put my hand into his, though I didn't need help standing.

Krisbaum rejoined us, saying, "I had a look. The rangers—or whatever the hell they are—are doing okay, keeping people away. But jeez, you think they'da known better than to move the guy!"

I wanted to know where LaVoq had died and where he was now, but I didn't ask. Surgelato was scowling at his watch with beetle-browed impatience. He was through talking to me.

It was time to meet the Merced police.

18

IT TOOK ME four hours to explain the situation to the Merced police. An apple-cheeked detective kept interrupting my litany about Bud Hopper to ask irrelevant questions about how I'd passed my morning. Later, a stocky cop in a baseball jersey accompanied me to my room so I could show him my snapshot of LeVoq. I sagely advised him to ask room service if they'd delivered a similar parcel to anyone else in the hotel. The detective, however, had obviously never read Nancy Drew; he did not appreciate brilliant amateurs.

When the cops were finally through with me, I went looking for Surgelato and Krisbaum, but they'd vanished like wood nymphs. I was back in my room staring at my document-strewn bed when Melinda Karastatos knocked on my door. She staggered in, collapsing into the Navajo-upholstered chair.

She moaned, "I politicked against him, but I *liked* him. I mean, if he hadn't been my boss, I'd have liked him."

I carefully gathered up the documents and tucked them into my vinyl briefcase. I wanted a leather case; really *wanted* one, all of a sudden.

"I didn't want him to *die*!" Melinda continued, unknotting the bow of her white silk blouse.

I watched her. Why did people have to talk about it? Why couldn't they leave their grief—*my* grief—alone? "Who . . . found him?"

She clutched the ends of her shambled bow. "I don't know. I was in the lobby when they carried him in. He looked—all *dirty*." I'd never heard the word spoken quite that way before; it plumbed the depths of amazed disgust.

"What was he wearing?"

"Wearing?" She seemed a little annoyed; we were here to praise Caesar, not discuss his clothes. "A red shirt, I think."

I sat on the bed beside my briefcase. The last time I'd seen Bob LeVoq, he'd just pulled a red polo shirt over his head. Had he left my room and gone directly to meet his maker?

Poison hemlock can take hours to catch up with its victim. Julian Warneke had returned to the office after his fatal lunch and worked until five o'clock.

Two bosses poisoned. Wouldn't *that* look great on my résumé?

When I looked at Melinda again, she was weeping. Her shoulders and chest convulsed, but she cried quietly, not troubling to hide her teary face. I lamely commented that everyone knew she'd liked Bob. And was mercifully interrupted by a knock at the door.

Hannah Crosby stood in the corridor, her fine-featured face white beneath its paint. Flyaway wisps of hair had broken free of her tortoise-shell comb, and she smoothed them back with a long, loving caress. She wore a belted polka-dot dress that might possibly have worked for Marilyn Monroe.

She stepped inside, slammed the door shut, and got the worst case of the shakes I've ever seen. In a tone as piercing as a boiling crab's, she shrieked, "It won't work!"

I assumed she referred to the suppression of her grief. I was therefore surprised when she took three furious strides across the room and loomed threateningly over the seated Melinda. "It *won't work*!" she repeated. "Pablo is no fool!"

Melinda seemed to know what Hannah was talking about, because she retorted, "Neither is Bill!"

I wasn't sure how our respective bosses figured into the discussion, but then, I didn't know what we were discussing.

Hannah backed abruptly toward the bed and sat down; almost as though Melinda had done it telekinetically. She said, "I *know* why it happened!"

Melinda wiped away tears, snapping, "You always *know* everything!"

"He and Colin—"

And William Mott rapped loudly on the door, identifying himself as he knocked. It was such a jolly party; all it lacked was Bill Mott.

He managed to look dignified in madras slacks and a navy blue Izod. "Is Melinda here?" he inquired.

His question was merely a display of manners, as Melinda was visible from the doorway.

I didn't have time to say yes before Melinda flew past me and into Mott's arms.

She was four inches taller and at least twenty years younger than Mott, but her embrace was more than just collegial.

I looked away. I was embarrassed by the look on Mott's pruney face as he clutched her to his hollow chest, his eyes tightly closed.

I glanced at Hannah Crosby. She was blinking at them with complete, unfeigned astonishment. Then she looked at me. When our eyes met, we did something shamefully gauche. We giggled.

Melinda and Mott immediately unclenched, as if we'd turned a garden hose on them.

Mott mumbled something about a meeting, and he and Melinda hurried away down the corridor together.

I closed the door, and turned back to Hannah Crosby. We were still laughing convulsively—neurotically— when my next visitor arrived.

19

THE NEWCOMER LOOKED like some kind of confection, from her butterscotch curls to a ruffled dress that might have been applied with a frosting syringe.

Hannah Crosby choked back a final peal of unseemly laughter, wiping tears and makeup from her cheeks. "Mrs. LeVoq!"

I stood in the middle of the room, hiccoughing and blinking at the woman who'd just flung open my door.

Mrs. LeVoq, less sweet of tongue than of aspect, spat

out, "You *camp follower*! I should have known you'd be here!"

The young widow obviously understood the nature of Hannah's relationship to LeVoq. I hoped she didn't mean to communicate the extent of her knowledge in my presence, however.

I stepped closer to Mrs. LeVoq, noticing the pout lines chiseled into her forehead and under her mouth. Her cornflower eyes glinted, but not with tears.

"I'm Willa Jansson." I blocked her view of Hannah Crosby, thrusting out my hand for shaking. "You must be very upset. Can I order something for you from—"

She pushed past me. "You thought I didn't know about you and Bob!"

Judging from Hannah's face, Mrs. LeVoq was correct.

"Well, I did know!" The widow's tone said, *Take that*. "I knew about all his women!" *And that*.

Hannah Crosby looked mildly chagrined; no more. She shifted in her chair, smoothing her polka dots to minimize sit wrinkles. "Have you been here long?" she asked politely. "I didn't see you last night at dinner."

Mrs. LeVoq seemed to deflate, folding slowly until she sat on my bed. From halfway across the room, I could smell talcum powder. "I couldn't get a sitter until this morning."

Kids. Bob LeVoq might have been a good father, boisterous and full of teasing mischief. Or he might have been too self-centered to pay attention to his offspring. Either way, they'd probably loved him. I leaned against a wall, praying Mrs. LeVoq wouldn't talk about them anymore.

Hannah Crosby apparently did not share my desire. "Are the children provided for?" she inquired, with the coolness of a social service employee.

"Of course!" Mrs. LeVoq's jelly-bean blue eyes glinted with outrage. "Bob was always very good about—"

"He was well insured, presumably?"

I had to admire Hannah; never in my Nancy Drewest dreams would I have asked such a question. Conducting fiscal strip-searches must toughen bank officers.

"Among other things!" Mrs. LeVoq's handbag slid from her peach sateen lap. I was surprised to see the bag was vinyl. Had LeVoq kept her short of cash? "Does it make your conscience feel better to know that?"

"My conscience?" Hannah smiled slightly, as if the very idea amused her. "I was merely concerned. As a friend—"

"A friend! You call yourself my—"

"—of Robert's. Wailes, Roth has the usual sort of insurance, I imagine? A quarter of a million accidental death, with double indemnity if the accident occurs during a work-related—"

"That's none of your business!" Mrs. LeVoq's voice shook; she was as angry as she had a right to be. "*Who* do you think you are?"

Whoever Hannah Crosby thought she was, she wasn't ashamed of it. "That would be the standard policy. Perhaps Wailes is more generous."

Mrs. LeVoq frowned as if discovering a new species of cockroach. "If you're thinking of trying to get *palimony*, or something like that—"

"I'm not hard up, Betty."

"Bonnie—as if you didn't know."

"Bonnie"—she glanced over her shoulder at the sudden bustle of waiters on the path outside my window—"it strikes me that you don't seem very sad."

"Of all the— I suppose *you're* sadder than me!"

Hannah laughed, a two-second unamused kind of laugh. "You're absolutely right, Betty—Bonnie. If we went by appearances, Melinda Karastatos would seem to be Bob's chief mourner."

20

THE WHOLE BUNCH of them gave me the creeps. William Mott revealing wizened lust for Melinda; Hannah Crosby handling LeVoq's widow with the tact of a Freddy Krueger; the L.A. partners meeting in the spa to compose a notice that "despite the sad, senseless loss of an esteemed partner" the networking and power kayaking would continue.

All I wanted to do was go home.

Melinda, minus her aging paramour, tried to dissuade me. "We're in a spot. We need L.A.'s goodwill more than ever!" She stood at my window, looking out at the wilderness-black night. "We're a small office to begin with—an offshoot." She turned to me, fiercely shaking dust out of the curtain. "If they cool off to us now—or if our clients do—we're through. We've got to go downstairs and show L.A. we're worth saving!" Her cheeks flamed, her brows pinched under disheveled bangs. "L.A.'s going to have to help us solidify our client base—Bill Mott's been trying, but he needs help.

We've got to show L.A.—starting tonight!—that we're worth their effort. That the San Francisco associates have the Stuff''—verbally capitalized—''to make the office a blockbuster!''

I felt like I was being recruited for the Marine Corps. But however badly it reflected on my *esprit*, my two-handled paper Macy's bag was packed, and would remain packed. And if I ever succeeded in finding Don Surgelato and Danny Krisbaum (I'd been all over the hotel forty times, looking for them), I'd beg them for a ride home. If worse came to worst, I'd wait for the morning Greyhound. But no way would I spend the evening of my boss's murder networking.

"You know," Melinda added huskily, "they *might* just give us severance pay and say 'so long.' ''

"They wouldn't—''

"It's a small office," she reiterated. "And Bob was its manager—supposedly.''

I thought about my ninety thousand dollars a year. The new couch and TV I hadn't yet had a chance to buy. The leather briefcase.

"This is the critical juncture, Willa! *Right now*, believe me!'' Her voice shook with sincerity; there was no doubting her. "They're going to decide this weekend—subliminally, anyway—whether to pull the plug on our office!''

Two bosses in a row murdered. I'd never find another ninety-thousand-dollar job.

"What can *we* do?'' I mumbled grudgingly.

"Dazzle them. Go down to dinner and be properly sorry and properly subdued, but also dazzle them with our brilliance and our commitment to making the office a top-biller.''

Didn't *that* sound like a relaxing evening.

Melinda seemed to sense that I was wavering. She hit below the belt. "There's the support staff to think

of, too. If we go, so do Jaclyn, Rhonda, Brigid and
McNee.''

I swore quietly as I shook the wrinkles out of my one
and only silk dress.

21

I WAS SEATED between William Mott and a corpulent
man who introduced himself as the World Financial
Network. Mott seemed particularly anxious that the
man sit beside me. Judging from the man's straying
glances, he'd have preferred to sit beside the back-
less—and nearly frontless—women of Excelsior Pro-
ductions.

Mott told him, ''Willa will be assisting Melinda on
your case, Hugo.''

I smiled at Hugo—dazzlingly, I hoped.

And he looked at me the way Julian Warneke's Team-
ster clients used to look at me. I almost expected him
to echo the sentiments of one union man: This broad's
spost to be my *lawyer*?

Mott continued amiably, ''You'll find the case very

interesting, Willa. Over the course of a year, WFN lent close to fifteen million to Malhousie Law School.'' He waited for me to react to the mention of my alma mater. I didn't. ''Malhousie, as you may know, wants to tear down a number of residence hotels in the Tenderloin area and build a new library complex.''

''There's a lawsuit, isn't there, halting demolition?'' My parents and their usual coalition of old left, new labor and radical clergy had helped stall eviction of the tenants—most of them seniors or boat people—until the suit could be filed. They'd done it the usual way, by laying their bodies across hotel thresholds and Tenderloin streets.

''Could be a year before the matter's settled,'' Hugo muttered crossly. ''We're calling in the loan, of course.''

Social Darwinism in action. ''I gather Malhousie wants to hang on to the money until it can start building?'' I took a sip of the wine; it tasted like sour mold. Across from me, two partners went into raptures over it, in spite of its ''case price'' of only forty dollars a bottle.

Hugo shrugged. ''They're countersuing. We expected it.''

''Melinda is deposing Dean Grenville on Wednesday, I believe,'' Mott interjected.

I choked on my wine. ''Milton Grenville?''

The World Financial Network, apparently bored by this discussion, turned to the person on his left. Mott murmured, ''Did you have a class from him?''

''Criminal procedure.'' The misswallowed red wine seared my eustachian tubes. Milton Grenville, among the most pompous and opinionated of Malhousie's professors (quite a distinction, given the competition), now headed a citizen's action committee to which my parents belonged.

When he wasn't evicting boat people from Tenderloin hotels, he was chairing the Suspend Surgelato Committee.

Sean Kowalski, sunburnt after a day of kayaking, called across the table that there would be dancing later. I hate dancing. I'm not graceful and it irritates me that I'm not supposed to lead.

Depressing to think dinner would be the "fun" part of my evening.

I was seated at the front of the candle-lit dining hall with my back to the assembly, and I could feel people staring at me. Whenever I glanced over my shoulder, eyes were averted. Once, I saw myself pointed out from across the room. They wondered if I'd killed Bob LeVoq.

Melinda's admonitions aside, the minute dinner ended, I ran to my room and repacked my bag.

In the morning, I was going home. Ninety thousand a year be damned.

22

I SHOULD HAVE known what I'd find at home. Enterprising reporters had discovered I worked for Bob LeVoq. It had been only six months since the similar demise of my prior boss; and unfortunately (in this respect), Warneke's killer had been shot before the media could feast upon a lurid murder trial. Reporters now looked to me for the high drama of which they'd earlier been cheated.

They banged on my door, they phoned me, they camped on my front and back doorsteps, and they interviewed my landlord (who lost no time alerting them to the perfidies of the Trilateral Commission). I knew I'd have to find temporary asylum somewhere.

My old room, with its Grateful Dead and Big Brother posters, remained trapped in amber at my parents' flat. It wasn't uncommon for me to sleep there a couple of nights a month.

But I surveyed the stack of books my father had left on my coffee table. The tottering heap represented my

parent's attempt at subtle persuasion. Their flat was
lined with walls of paperback revolution; the Kremlin
library, a friend had called it. And my parents would
inflict it on me like a Chinese water torture—an epi-
gram here, a dialectic there—if I went to their place.
They (especially Mother) would feel duty-bound to res-
cue me from the murky depths of respectability. She
would strive to rehabilitate my politics with the fervor
of a missionary saving souls.

I didn't want to be deprogrammed. I just wanted to
sell out in peace.

I fumbled through a desk drawer full of loose change
and leaky pens until I found what I was looking for: a
duplicate key to Julian Warneke's house. When Mother
inherited the house, we expected a probate challenge
from Warneke's children. So far, none had occurred.
The neighbors, on the other hand, had all but fire-
bombed the place. Having met the paroled sociopaths
Mother installed there, I didn't blame them.

Nevertheless, I decided to take my chances at Mother's newly formed "commune." It had to be better than
coping with my parental Gang of Two.

At least, I thought so until I got there.

23

IT WAS A two-story plaster building, gray with white bas-relief ribbons between the windows. It shared walls with a renovated Victorian on one side, and a wood-shingled modern on the other. Half a block away, behind a blizzard of traffic, was a landscaped strip of lawn separating the bay from the Marina District.

San Franciscans love their bay—as a view from Pacific Heights or Telegraph Hill. But you don't often see them standing beside it; they maintain an urbane distance, lingering in Marina District bars, their feet firmly planted on polished oak as they pry open oysters and listen to sound buoys. It's mostly tourists who mosey and Frisbee along the grass strip, photographing their windswept families against a background of bridge traffic. But something about the neighborhood—the glimpse of bay from top floor apartments, the tourist dollars, the chichi night life—had made Julian Warneke's (now my mother's) modest three-bedroom house worth three quarters of a million dollars.

I pulled my bag up Warneke's—Mother's—alabaster steps and rang the bell. A brass plate warned me that I stood at the threshold of A Fresh Start Commune. One of Mother's two communards ("Not *tenants*—you know I'd never be a *landlord*, baby!") flung open the front door. He glowered at me, fists clenched, cheek muscles twitching. No wonder neighbors wanted the place down-zoned to a single-family dwelling.

"Mr. Poat? I'm Willa Jansson. We met a few weeks ago."

I'd helped Mother fill out the papers required by Justin Poat's parole board. After six years of quiet toil as a bank teller, Poat had one day carried a pipe bomb to work in his briefcase. When the bomb failed to explode, he pulled it out of the briefcase and attacked a bank officer with it. The bank officer, Mother informed me bitterly, came out of it with nothing but a few stitches in the scalp. "Poor Justin," on the other hand, served seven years for aggravated assault.

As he stood before me now, the gray bags under his eyes throbbed, his lower lip pulled stiffly away from his teeth, and he made unconscious back-off gestures with his hands. Easy to see why Mother had loved him at first sight.

I added rather nervously, "Don't you remember me? June Jansson's daughter?" I shifted my shopping bag and extended my right hand.

Poat didn't shake it. He backed hastily away from the door, flailing his arms. His eyes, the only imposing thing about the stringy little man, burned with a tele-vangelist zeal. "What do you want here?" Dirty brown hair straggled over his forehead. "Who sent you?"

A caftaned waif floated to his side. She was probably the only human being within a hundred miles who was paler than Poat. Her long, plain face was scarred at the forehead, crinkling one of her thin brows. Her eyelids and nose were red. Amanda McGuire had recently served two years for felony child abuse.

"Hi, Mandy," I said. "You remember me, don't you?"

She nodded meekly. I think she'd have agreed with anything I said. I'd spent two months in the San Bruno jail myself; I'd seen it do that to some women.

"There's no one in the third bedroom right now, is there?" I stepped inside. "I need to crash here for a couple of days."

Poat twitched. Mandy blinked.

"I won't disturb you," I promised. I wondered how they planned to spend the evening—Thorazine cocktails for two?

Poat stuttered, "I'm c-calling your mother!"

Mandy trudged toward me, slurring, "You must be hungry. I'll cook you some dinner." She sounded like a 45 played at 33.

Before I could dissuade her, she'd sleepwalked away toward the kitchen.

Poat was in the middle of another "back-off" pantomime, his lips curled as if he'd tasted poison. To this he added a compulsive shaking of the head, and a noise that sounded like "Gnaaagh! Gnaaagh!" I was having serious doubts about my welcome.

Finally Poat wheeled around and ran into the hall.

I dropped my Macy's bag and looked around. When Warneke's widow lived here, the hardwood floors had gleamed, and the monastery-style furniture had been carefully arranged and oiled.

Now, a shaft of sunlight from the bay window caught the swirl of dust rising from the Goodwill couch. The oak floors had been scrubbed to dullness. The walls were bare of everything except kitchen-towel calendars. On them, bluebirds fluttered and nineteenth-century gents took sleigh rides. They weren't my mother's style; they had to be Amanda's. On a particle-board coffee table were two of the stalking, red-eyed china panthers everyone owned in 1959. Between them was a cheap glass candy dish filled with jawbreakers and loose change. On the floor beside a sprung recliner were several back issues of *TV Guide*. There was no television in the room. The overall effect was of malfunctioning androids trying to play house.

Poat reentered the room. ''Your mother says you can stay here.''

Mandy, appearing suddenly in the doorway, burst into tears.

''Stop it!'' Poat ordered.

She stopped it, wiping her eyes on an East Indian print sleeve. ''They won't let *my* daughter stay.''

''You beat her up every time you see her!'' Poat snapped. Then I thought he muttered something about a bad credit history. Maybe my job was getting to me.

''Don't change your routine on my account!'' I insisted. ''I'll be at work most of the time, anyway. I've got a house key, so I won't need you to answer the door—''

''I'll keep your dinner warm,'' Mandy said contritely.

''No! Really. I'll be grabbing something at work most nights—''

''You'll have stress.'' She blinked worriedly. ''Viruses come when you have stress.''

''I'll be all right.'' My stress level was bound to plunge when I left the house each morning.

''You're not a banker, are you?'' Poat asked suspiciously.

''No!'' I decided not to mention I was a bank lawyer.

''You want to know what they do in banks?'' Poat stepped closer. I could smell his breath, sharp and sour.

''Maybe after I get settled!'' I dashed into the corridor and up the stairs.

Luckily, Mother had furnished the third, still uninhabited bedroom. It was cheerfully Latin American, with a woven Guatemalan bedspread on a lumpy old bed. On the walls were stylized paintings of birds, tempera on birch bark. A Spanish-English phrase book and Spanish-language bible were on the nightstand.

And knowing Mother, I understood why the room was empty. She had no intention of finding a third parolee-boarder. She had reserved the room for Salvadoran refugees passing through on the underground railroad. I wondered if Mandy and Justin were aware of Mother's plan—and that its illegality violated the terms of their parole.

24

AN UNCOMFORTABLE NIGHT on a lumpy bed, and housemates who stayed up until the wee hours pacing (in Justin's case) and scouring floors (in Mandy's case), were almost enough to make me look forward to another day of work.

That was before I ran into Colin Aasgar. He was perched on the receptionist's desk, a fifteen-foot semicircle of pink marble. The desk was ringed with baskets of out-of-season flowers, and Aasgar had cleared a spot beside Jaclyn's chair. Jaclyn had a Louis Vuitton makeup case in her lap. Amid the flowers, she and Aasgar looked like the bride and groom, about to leave the reception.

I glanced at a card nestled in a silver bucket of gladiolas. *With deep sadness at the loss of a fine lawyer and good friend.* Signed Marty Wein, Florence, Italy.

Jaclyn stated the obvious: "They're for Bob." Her face was rigid with the effort of remaining tearless. Judging by the size of her makeup bag, repairs would have been a major project.

Aasgar didn't bother greeting me. He watched an overalled man cross the reception area toward us, wheeling a dolly stacked with file boxes.

"Bob's papers?" I felt subdued, watching LeVoq ebb out of the office in so tangible a manner.

"Mine," Aasgar drawled. Then louder, to the man, "Keep that steady!"

"Yours! Is the office—"

Aasgar snorted. "What office? Bob *was* this office!"

At the other end of the reception area, William Mott suddenly planted himself in front of the dolly. He yanked the lid off the topmost box, and, with a quick, furious gesture, commanded the mover to return the boxes to Aasgar's office.

Aasgar muttered, "Not on your life!" and met Mott in the middle of the room. They were surrounded by enough green carpet to give the impression of a duel in progress.

Mott said stiffly, "Client files remain in this office until such time—*if* it ever occurs—that the client instructs me to prepare a copy—a *copy*, not the original—for transfer to his new attorney of record."

"Dilatory tactics won't raise your stock with Transport Trust, Mott! And don't worry—you *will* be hearing from them!''

With a flick of the forefinger at Jaclyn, Aasgar stormed out of the office suite. Jaclyn, head bent, hoisted her makeup case over her shoulder and followed him.

Mott turned to glare at Brigid, Rhonda and McNee. The two young secretaries pretended to be busy. McNee walked airily to Jaclyn's desk and flipped a button on her telephone, which immediately rang. ''Law office,'' he said melodiously into the receiver. Then, ''We have no comment.'' He punched another button and said the same thing. It happened three or four more times before I roused myself to go talk to Melinda.

I passed the offices of the firm's other two attorneys, one a languid Harvard grad who preceded our every conversation with a superior snicker, and the other a chubby Columbia boy whose idea of pro bono work was preparing challenges to rent-control ordinances. Both their office doors were open. Both their offices were empty. No books on the shelves, no papers on the desks. Empty.

When Julian Warneke was murdered, no one deserted ship. We divvied up Julian's clients and kept plugging away on their behalf. And we weren't paid the moon to do it, like these people. Were their sensibilities really so fragile? Or were they so marketable they didn't have to consider anything except their own professional convenience?

A third possibility occurred to me. Maybe they assumed I was a homicidal maniac, indulging in killing sprees wherever I worked. Maybe the two young associates were afraid of me.

I tapped at Melinda's door. I expected to find her closeted with Mott, but she wasn't. She was sitting at her desk flipping through folders of pleadings as if trying to set a speed-reading record. Though it was cool in the temperature-controlled office, Melinda was sweating. Her bangs clung damply to her forehead and her linen shirt was unbuttoned at the throat and wrists.

She glanced up at me. "Thank god you're finally here."

It was eight-thirty. "The offices are empty."

"The baby lawyers"—her term for lawyers fresh out of law school—"cleared out this weekend."

"Because of—"

"LeVoq!" She spat the word. "He told everyone the office was folding! He had the *gall*"—her voice dropped to a tense, mannish rumble—"to try to woo away World Financial at the retreat! Right under our noses!"

"Did the baby lawyers give notice?"

She shook her head. "Melvin's over at Pillsbury, Madison this morning—god, they deserve each other! And Goren has some kind of clerkship lined up. Know how I found out?" She pulled a stiff white tabloid out from under a pile of folders. *"American Lawyer."*

The American Lawyer is a cross between *The Wall Street Journal* and *The National Enquirer*. It's a dignified, insider-oriented gossip-and-scandal sheet. Melinda opened it to an article whose headline proclaimed: WAILES, ROTH S.F. IN TROUBLE—SIX-PERSON OFFICE SHRINKS TO TWO.

"How did they find out about Bob in time to print—"

"They didn't. The article assumes Bob is alive—and opening an office with Colin Aasgar!"

I picked up the magazine, skimming quickly. The baby lawyers had provided quotes and information. Wailes, Roth's senior associate, they said, spent all her time bickering with partners and taking clients to lunch; as a result, the junior associates were burdened with all the actual work. Meanwhile, their allegiance to the San Francisco office was made "inefficacious" by the maneuverings of "certain Los Angeles partners," who were attempting to run the office from afar "as if by white magic." As a result, associates could never be sure who had final say on any given issue. And— apparently worst of all, judging from the bitterness of their quotes—a new attorney (me) had been lateraled in ahead of them, "significantly altering one's expectations of early partnership." This new lawyer, they complained, had no previous bank law experience, but was merely a "low-end tenants' rights/Legal Aid type." (Goddamned pampered preppies!)

No wonder Melinda looked murderous. "Why didn't they just give notice? Why give a splashy interview, then sneak out in the night?"

She just looked at me. She didn't have to say it. *LeVoq.*

"You think Bob put them up to it?"

"I phoned a friend of mine at Pillsbury this morning," she said through tight lips. "Bob gave Melvin a reference! He *knew* about this!" She snatched the tabloid away and slapped it onto the desktop. "It wasn't enough for Bob, prying away our clients. He was going to blast the office to atoms!"

"But why? He was a partner! He could have kept on collecting his paycheck while everyone else did the work for him."

"Oh, no," Melinda said venomously. "He was a lazy pile of shit, and the right people were finally catching on! The executive committee meeting next week—firing Bob was on the agenda."

"Firing a partner?" Partnership was supposed to be sacrosanct—the ultimate in job security.

" 'Firing a partner?' " Melinda mimicked. "More like fumigating a pestilence!" She flushed to the roots of her hair. "I'm sorry! I keep forgetting that he's . . . !" She dropped her face into her hands and her shoulders shook, whether from exhaustion or tears I didn't know.

Through her fingers she muttered, "Where the *hell* did I put those Transport files?"

I remembered Bob LeVoq foisting the Transport Trust case on Melinda the day of my interview. Since then, I'd heard her complain she was spending forty hours a week on that case alone. I didn't think she was going to like what I had to say. "The files were just wheeled into Bill Mott's office."

She dropped her hands from her face. No tears. "Wheeled?"

"On a dolly. Colin was having his stuff moved out—"

"Colin! Transport is *my* case!" Furiously, she punched some buttons on her telephone. "Where does Colin get off—Bill?" she barked into her speaker. "Is Transport Trust in your office?"

There was a short silence. Then a wary, "Yes."

Melinda waved me out of the room. Before the door closed, I heard Mott interrupt her tirade against Colin.

"I just talked to the client, Melinda. Transport's board of directors has voted to remove us as counsel of record." I held the door open long enough to hear Mott add, "They voted last week. They replaced us with the firm of LeVoq and Aasgar. They were surprised Bob didn't tell us."

25

"WILL YOU SEE me?"

Don Surgelato didn't answer immediately. I pressed the telephone receiver more firmly to my ear. I couldn't hear him breathing. Maybe he'd put me on hold again.

"Is it directly relevant to the LeVoq investigation?"

Directly relevant—he sounded like a goddamn lawyer. "Indirectly relevant. Office gossip."

"The LeVoq investigation is not in my jurisdiction. You should phone the Merced police."

"That's a long-distance call."

"A fifty-cent toll. And you're making ninety grand a year."

"Not for long. The office is collapsing. That's what I want to talk to you about."

"Merced," he said flatly. "Area code two oh nine. Three eight five six nine one two."

"I don't want to talk to Merced."

"Then I'll have them call you." He hung up.

He'd been willing to talk to me at the Mariposa. What the hell had happened since then?

Andrew McNee slid into my office like the perfect butler, not bothering to knock. He deposited a stack of letters on my desk and replaced the telephone receiver I'd smacked down on the desk blotter. "The temporary receptionist has arrived," he said with some asperity. "If he misdirects your phone calls, please inform me so that I can let his agency know. Not," he added, "that we're likely to find anyone better today." He bent forward confidingly, even a little campily. "Neither of our usual temps could be persuaded to come!"

"Why not?" Mourning for LeVoq? A horror of publicity? Knowledge that the phones would ring constantly?

He shrugged. "The reporters, I suppose."

"Are they being a nuisance?"

McNee's lips curled. I wouldn't call it a smile. "I'll say this much for our temp: he's been quite efficient in turning them away. Thank goodness for that, anyway."

A few hours later, Rhonda buzzed me and deferentially ordered me to William Mott's office. "He'd like to see you right now, if you're not in conference."

As I crossed the acre of green carpet, I glimpsed the temporary receptionist. He was young, ruddy and a little stout. I stopped, watching him jot down a telephone message.

His name was Kelly. I knew that because he'd questioned me some months ago, in connection with Julian Warneke's murder. He was a San Francisco Police Homicide Inspector. So much for Surgelato's crap about jurisdiction.

Kelly saw me watching him. Impassively, he waited to see what I would do. I nodded distantly, as if to a stranger, and continued on to Mott's office.

As soon as I knocked, Mott opened his door. His eyes looked tiny without his usual magnifying glasses.

His brows were pinched and he rubbed his throat nervously. I wondered if he knew our receptionist was a cop.

I also wondered if Kelly was there to protect us or surveil us.

Mott took hold of my elbow, drawing me into his office. He seemed relieved to close the door. He motioned me into a chair, fiddling briefly with the doorknob. For a paranoid instant, I thought he'd locked it. But watching him cross the room, I dismissed the notion. His shoulders drooped, caving in his wizened chest. His skin looked clammy in the white-sky light from his wall of window. He looked old and exhausted. There was nothing menacing about him except his intellect.

He stepped behind his desk. "What case are you working on now?"

"Peninsula Mercedes-Jaguar got a court order compelling Bank of—"

"Put it aside." He sank into his cloud of leather, rubbing his knuckles over his lips. As "managing" partner, he'd invested his reputation in the success of the San Francisco office. Its disintegration, even more than LeVoq's murder, was bound to lower his stock in L.A. and in New York. No wonder he wasn't in fine fettle. "I want you to take over the World Financial case."

"Against *Malhousie*?" I tried not to sound hysterical, but I didn't want to sue my law school. I didn't want to face my professors again. Particularly now that I was embroiled in another murder case.

And what would my mother say if I represented the money behind demolition of her pet low-rent hotels?

"Isn't that Melinda's case?" I asked hopefully.

"Yes." He glanced at the closed office door. "It *was*. I want you to take over."

"You mean work with her?"

"You'll have sole responsibility."

"Will Melinda do the actual trial? It's a fifteen-million-dollar case, isn't it?"

"That's the amount owing on the loan. But Malhousie claims a hundred million in damages resulting from the bank's refusal to extend additional credit." He let it sink in: not a fifteen-million-dollar case—a hundred-million-dollar case. "But you've had trial experience—"

"One trial! On a very simple legal issue." I couldn't believe Mott wanted to throw me into a hundred-million-dollar lawsuit, sink or swim, all alone. "I have no commercial litigation experience! None whatsoever."

"You'll do fine." There was a disembodied quality to his words; they were uninflected, as if he didn't mean them but was committed to speaking them anyway. "You'll have to put in a late night—I'm afraid you have a deposition tomorrow. Malhousie's dean of financial affairs—"

I groaned audibly. Dean Milton Grenville had formerly presided over (without actually managing to teach) criminal procedure. I'd spent three months listening to him cloak a left-wing civil liberties stance in the rhetoric of conservative case analysis. He was also well known for his scholarly essays disdaining the death penalty on legal (not moral) grounds.

In addition to being a liberal in conservative's clothing, he was the chairman and legitimizing force behind the Suspend Surgelato Committee. His hawk-featured, bow-tied outrage photographed well on the Channel Two News.

William Mott slid a stack of files and transcripts across his desk. "Tomorrow's deposition precedes our document request. Your main object at this point is to get Grenville on record regarding what he did with WFN's money. We'll have an army of auditors go through Malhousie's books after you get the court orders, so don't worry about establishing concealment and comingling. For now, just try to pin Grenville down so we can contradict him later with the results of the audit. The fact that you were once his student may actually encourage him to bluff and bluster a bit—to underestimate us and say more than he should.'' Mott didn't look convinced. ''At the very least, have him state for the record that he didn't comingle. . . . ''

He examined my face as if searching for signs of intelligence. His mouth tightened as if someone were turning invisible screws. He shook his head slightly. If he didn't consider me equal to the task, why was he turning the case over to me?

''Does Melinda have too many other things to do?''

''We've lost four attorneys,'' he said bleakly. ''I'll attempt to lateral some people in, but . . .'' He burrowed deeper into his chair. ''A great deal depends on California Bank and Trust. Whether they are willing to remain with us.''

26

I APPROACHED MALHOUSIE reluctantly. A fine dust covered its alabaster stairs, coagulating in sticky corners. Across the street, in place of the dreary hotel I remembered, bulldozers swarmed around steel struts, and pile-drivers boomed like the telltale heart. Apparently Malhousie had managed to spend some of World Financial's money.

In the dark lobby, I displayed my bar association membership card for a uniformed guard. Behind him, students pressed toward the cafeteria, grumbling and laughing, stuffing papers into casebooks. The smell of ancient gravy wafted over them.

I pushed through the crowd toward the stairs, pausing at a row of engraved plaques on the wall. *Order of the Coif*, they proclaimed—an august way of saying, "Top Ten Percent." I walked past eighty-eight years' worth of tiny names before finding mine: Willa June Jansson, 1985. Julian Warneke had insisted I "make Coif," so he could sell me to partners who didn't think they could afford another attorney. I recognized other names on the list: mostly classmates I'd disliked—outliners and résumé-boosters. And now, like them, I was a bank lawyer. It was like finding my name on the Vietnam Veterans Memorial Wall.

I hit the stairs. The jostling of students, the smell of post-racquetball cologne, the scrape of Reeboks and wingtips and high-heeled pumps on the traction strips, the bandied names of professors—I felt a wave of relief: whatever else might befall me, law school was over.

Upstairs, I found Dean Grenville's reception room packed with my old professors.

I paused in the doorway, horrified. My consumer credit and conveyancing professors pushed past me, taking no notice of me. That left evidence, civil procedure, and federal income tax (the sight of whom sent a stab of pain to my left brain).

The men stood before an unoccupied desk, speaking simultaneously and waving copies of a thin tabloid I recognized as *The Malhousie Law News*. My evidence professor glanced at me, then continued trying to make his keening voice heard over civil procedure's bellow and income tax's rasp. He was saying, "Libel is a two-edged sword! Not only would it be unpopular within the student body—" He stopped, looked momentarily stunned, then looked at me again.

The sleek weasel of a law professor snapped, "Malhousie can't be in the position of funding yellow journalistic—" He followed the evidence professor's astonished gaze, and stopped.

That left only the civil procedure professor, booming into the sudden silence. "Student opinion is not the issue! It's the board of directors we need to—" The evidence professor gripped his arm, nodding toward me.

The power to deprive law professors of speech—I wish I'd developed it years earlier.

"Is Dean Grenville in?"

"You're Willa Jansson," the evidence professor grunted suspiciously.

He seemed to expect a hostile reply. *What's it to you?* perhaps. Or, *Who wants to know?* I wished I could oblige him. "Yes. I was in your evidence class."

"My evidence—" There'd been a hundred and ten students in that class; apparently it was my picture in the newspapers he remembered, not my scholarly presence in row seven.

"I'm with Wailes, Roth, Fotheringham and Beck now. I'm here to depose Dean Grenville."

The civil procedure professor glanced at his watch, frowning. "I represent the dean." He seemed to draw strength from his Rolex. When he looked at me again it was with squared shoulders and a complacent smile. "We were expecting Ms. Karastatos."

"Is the dean in?"

"Malhousie has retained outside counsel. Millet, Wray and Weissel. The dean is still at their office. You'll have to wait."

If there was a piggier firm than Wailes, Roth it was certainly Millet, Wray. They even had (I'd been told by friends who interviewed there) suede-walled offices.

The three professors watched me, obviously expecting a verbal reaction. I considered, *I haven't got all day, damn it*. But I did have all day. There was a chair beside me. I sat in it.

The professors moved their party out to the corridor. A moment later, a flustered young woman stepped out of Grenville's office, nearly shrieking at the sight of me. "Oh! I thought everyone was gone!" She looked at the door through which the professors had departed, and then glanced back at me dubiously.

She was a fluffy-haired, pink-cheeked woman in a drapy dress. She reminded me of a Macy's ad for The Larger Woman—well-proportioned and elegantly attired, but decidedly on the ample side. I wondered why she'd been hiding in the dean's office.

I told her who I was and why I was there.

Every hint of fluff vanished. Her hands tensed into modified fists (no use breaking perfect nails), and the look on her face could have kindled firewood.

I picked up a copy of *The Law News* from beneath my feet, and hid behind it. The headline read, DEAN OF FINANCE CAUGHT DIPPING INTO TILL. It was all I could do not to exclaim, "Oh goody!"

The dean walked in before I could read any farther. I slipped the paper into my briefcase and stood to greet him.

He looked me up and down, shaking his head impatiently. "You're not Ms. Karastatos." A narrow, hawk-nosed face and disordered puff of orange hair made him look like an ill-tempered woodpecker.

"I'm handling the deposition today." I managed to keep an aggrieved whine out of my voice, but just barely. My first deposition and I was up against Millet, Wray & Weissel. I fished in my suit pocket for a business card.

Grenville contemptuously flicked lint off it, then handed it to a towering gentleman behind him. The Millet, Wray lawyer was at least a foot taller than me, square-jawed, suntanned and poker-faced. I could see the comb marks in his blond hair. He looked like a cyborg in an expensive suit.

Grenville continued, "Jansson. You are an alumna, I believe." He sounded even less glad of the fact than I was.

"I was in your criminal procedure class in 1984."

He cast a bemused glance over his shoulder. The cyborg regarded me with eyes he might have purchased from a taxidermist.

"I suppose you've retained separate counsel, Dean?" I asked sweetly.

Grenville scowled, his skin blotching. He'd been the legal shepherd of World Financial Network's fifteen million: If judgment were entered against Malhousie, it could turn around and sue Grenville for any portion of the damages attributable to his mismanagement. And if the dean was guilty of more than mere mismanagement—if he'd comingled World Financial's money with his own discretionary accounts and then dipped into the till (as *The Law News* headline suggested) to finance junkets or entertaining expenses—he might find Malhousie filing criminal charges.

And I'd reminded him of it. Being a lawyer does have its moments.

"Professor Butler will join us shortly in that capacity," Grenville snarled. "I hope you don't mean to take up much of our day, Ms. Jansson."

I remembered Mott's hope that Grenville would underestimate me. "I honestly don't know. This is my first deposition."

Professor Butler entered as I spoke, his haughty smile convincing me that he, at least, had no trouble underestimating me. Perhaps he remembered my performance in first-year civil procedure.

The four of us marched funereally down the hall to the conference room, where a court reporter—hired by them and approved by us—sat ready to transcribe our every utterance.

Because of me, she ended up transcribing hours of nit-picking, probably irrelevant detail about the dean's duties: a description of accounts to which he was a signatory, a description of accounts to which he had no access ("or was supposed to have no access"), a description of Malhousie's fiscal hierarchy and his place in it. Then I went through World Financial's copy of Malhousie's loan application, point by point. What did you understand this to mean? Do you recall initialing this clause? Is this your signature here at the bottom?

These preliminaries took almost five hours. The idea of a deposition is to discover—and get on record—everything and anything that might bear on the litigation. Since I didn't know anything about the lawsuit, I had to err on the side of overkill. Even so, I was nervous as hell, afraid I'd neglect some seemingly unimportant question that would later make or break our case. Damn William Mott, anyway.

It was two o'clock and Grenville, white-lipped and testy, was fidgeting with hunger. At any moment, the Millet, Wray lawyer would demand a lunch break. I needed to get Grenville on record now, before French cuisine and exquisite wine restored him.

I pulled *The Malhousie Law News* out of my briefcase and laid it headline up on the table between us. "As dean of financial affairs, are you entitled to make this kind of personal withdrawal from a discretionary fund?"

The dean's lawyer slapped his palm on the oiled conference table. At best, my question assumed facts not in evidence; at worst, it was slanderous. But before he could object on either ground, the dean, completely exasperated, snapped, "It wasn't World Financial's money I withdrew! It's still there—"

His lawyer grabbed his arm, objecting loudly to the question, while the Millet, Wray lawyer ordered the dean not to answer.

Grenville leaped out of his chair. He'd just admitted depositing some of WFN's money into an account from which he'd made personal withdrawals. He'd failed to stick to the five "acceptable" deposition answers: Yes, No, I don't know, I don't recall, and None of your fucking business.

The Millet, Wray lawyer also rose, calmly suggesting a one-hour lunch.

As the court reporter put away her fanfold stack of papers, Grenville fumbled in his briefcase. He was scarlet-cheeked, a ridge of white curving over the cartilage of his nose. For a moment, I wondered if he had a gun in there. Instead, he pulled out a few sheets of paper, and slid them toward me across the table. The civil procedure professor would have snatched them up, but Grenville assured him, "A wholly unrelated matter."

I looked at the topmost sheet. In neat typeset boldface, a centered caption read, SUSPEND SURGELATO.

I blinked up at Grenville. As he said, a wholly unrelated matter. This hardly seemed the time or place to recruit me for his cause.

Grenville squinted down at me. "I'm given to understand that the lieutenant is romantically involved with you."

I shook my head numbly.

"Which casts his unprovoked assassination in a different light—"

"It was no assassination. And it wasn't unprovoked." I felt suddenly and stickily hot in my cheap suit.

Grenville's color was returning to normal. Bullying me was restoring his spirits. Professor Butler murmured something to him, trying to hustle him out of the room. Even the Millet, Wray cyborg looked a little nervous.

But Grenville was determined to best me. "The information regarding your possible liaison"—*possible;* not quite defamatory—"has been passed to the homicide team that investigated the assassination." He waited to see what effect this had on me, and I'm sure he wasn't disappointed. The shooting was investigated as a homicide? No wonder Surgelato hadn't returned my calls. "I'm confident," Grenville added nastily, "that it will result in a reopening of Civil Service Commission proceedings."

I stood up. "Your information is wrong. The lieutenant and I aren't romantically involved. We never have been.'' If the Civil Service Commission believed Surgelato killed a ''suspect'' to avenge the attempted murder of his sweetheart, he'd soon be out of work and under indictment. ''If you're trying to goad me into a slander suit so that Wailes, Roth has to withdraw from this—''

''What!'' he thundered. ''You think I'm afraid of a firm that sends an inexperienced young—!''

But the Millet, Wray lawyer stepped between us, requesting that I leave the conference room.

27

THE REST OF the deposition consisted mostly of ''I don't recall.'' Grenville couldn't have been more forgetful if he'd developed Alzheimer's.

Worse, I'd let him rattle me and we both knew it. He ostentatiously displayed his anti-Surgelato manifesto on the table between us (right next to my copy of *The Malhousie Law News*), and every time I glanced at it, I noticed phrases so shrill and flowery they could only have been penned by my mother. It didn't take Nancy

Drew to figure out who'd told Grenville that Surgelato and I were "romantically involved."

By six o'clock I was wishing I still washed dishes in a vegetarian restaurant. I climbed wearily into a cab, watching twilight change the neighborhood from almost-Civic-Center to downright Tenderloin. Business suits vanished into Marin-bound buses, replaced by wine-spattered overcoats and come-hither miniskirts.

"Where to?" the cabbie asked.

I knew I should go back to the office and talk to Mott about the deposition. I rubbed my temples. I didn't want to talk to Mott. And I didn't want to see Melinda. First Aasgar absconds with her biggest case, then Mott assigns her hundred-million-dollar baby to a rookie. Surely Mott was overly sanguine about her reaction. If Melinda really didn't mind, why hadn't she given me the case herself? Why hadn't she come to my office to talk about it?

"The meter's running, lady."

I gave the driver the address of the A Fresh Start Commune. I needed a joint. It might not be a fresh start, but it was all I could manage. I'd talk to Mott in the morning.

If I'd gone to my apartment instead of Mother's commune, I'd have learned I couldn't talk to Mott, ever again. Instead, I spent an evening in stoned (if not blissful) ignorance, watching Mandy dust the wainscoting, and listened to Justin catalogue every loan denied by the bank for which he'd once worked.

Stoned as I was, there was something fascinating about his passion for detail, even though I wasn't exactly sure what he was talking about.

"George E. Palmer doing business as Palmer Volkswagen," he hissed. "All he needed was a three-month float until the '80 models came in! Denied! Because of two lousy percentage points in his debt-to-equity ratio! And they'd just changed the ratio the week before because the housing market was rebounding and they needed more money for construction loans! One lousy week!'' His lank hair fanned down over his forehead. Gray pouches twitched beneath his eyes. ''And you know that chocolate chip cookie place on Jackson? The one where there's a line at lunchtime all the way down the block?'' He leaped to his feet, hands poised for a karate attack: the white-collar ninja. Mandy watched him, doe-eyed, her feather-duster hovering. ''They wouldn't lend the seed money for that, either! The *fools*!''

''I should make cookies!'' Mandy moaned.

''Cookies!'' Justin's arm snapped forward, karate-chopping the air a foot from her chin. ''I don't care about *cookies*!''

''Oh, no. I know that! Not for *you*.'' She looked aghast at the very idea of insulting him with cookies. ''For Willa.''

I smiled. She could insult me with cookies. Potheads go with the flow.

That was all the encouragement she needed to leave the living room and clatter around the kitchen. Justin began strutting. ''They put pubic hair in my food!'' he fumed. ''When I asked to go to the law library—one lousy hour a week—the lousy bastard of a guard reached into his pants and put his hair on my food!''

''Awful.'' I yawned, sinking deeper into the mildew-scented couch. In a town like San Francisco, you have to be stingy with your empathy or you end up like my mother.

''It would have been better if I'd blown us all up!'' he concluded bitterly.

Where was Daddy with his Martin Luther King and Henry Thoreau books now that I needed him?

When the doorbell buzzed, I thought maybe I'd managed to summon him astrally. Poat went white, staring into the hallway.

I sat up, preparing to answer the door.

Poat forestalled me, quavering, "No! *No! I'm* the man of the house." His hands shook so hard he had to tuck them under his armpits. Arms crossed over his chest, he disappeared into the hall. A full minute later I heard the creak of the door hinges, followed by a gasp. Then someone—Poat, presumably—sprinted down the hall and up the stairs.

I didn't want to see anyone. Especially someone who could send Poat scurrying upstairs that way.

I sat on the couch, blood pounding in my ears, expecting Dracula or the wolf man.

Instead, a florid and sweaty face popped into view, followed (with a grunt) by a hefty body in an unstylish brown suit.

"Inspector Krisbaum!" I wasn't sure whether to be relieved or alarmed. I wondered if he could smell pot smoke in the room.

"Who's the rabbit?" he asked me, pointing back toward the hall.

"Justin Poat. He's had some bad experiences with the law. I assume you showed him your badge?"

He nodded glumly.

"They used to put pubic hair in his food." I stifled a giggle.

"You okay, Miss Jansson?"

I looked up at him, feeling suddenly queasy. A draft brought in the smell of chocolate chip cookies baking. "You know, I went all day without thinking about Bob LeVoq. Isn't that bizarre?"

"Sheesh." He dropped into the sprung recliner. "Wish I could go half an hour without thinking about him."

"I thought the Merced police—"

"Not anymore. Tell me, where were you this afternoon?"

"Taking a deposition."

"What time did you get back to the office?"

I closed my eyes and tried to focus. What could have happened this afternoon? Krisbaum wouldn't care where I'd been unless—

"Who?"

"Who what?"

"Somebody else must be dead. That's why you're asking—"

"I'm asking"—he spoke slowly, with a hint of vexation—"because I want to know. What time did you go back to your office?"

"I didn't go back. I came here after the deposition."

"Why here? Why not your office?"

"I was tired."

"Why not your apartment, then?"

"I've been staying here the last couple of days to avoid reporters. How did you know about this place?"

"The lieutenant."

I nodded. Surgelato knew my mother had inherited it from Julian Warneke. He probably also knew she'd turned it into a boardinghouse for the misbegotten.

"What time did you get here, Miss Jansson?"

"I don't know. I caught a cab at around six-thirty."

"Where from?"

"The Civic Center."

"So you got here around ten to seven? Seven, maybe, with the traffic?"

"I'm not sure."

"Well, let's try to work it out. It's eight o'clock now. What did you do when you got back?"

Communed with my cannabis, but I wasn't about to admit it. "Flaked out."

He sniffed the air. "Yeah. Would your roommates know what time you got in?"

One of them chose that moment to step into the room with a plate of fresh cookies. She was singing, "Nothin' says lovin' like somethin' from the oven . . ." when

she caught sight of the burly detective. Everything about
her grew slack, her mouth, her cheek muscles, her
arms. The plate would have slid from her limp hands
to the floor if Krisbaum hadn't lunged forward to catch
it. I was surprised by his quickness; either he had great
reflexes or he loved cookies.

"It's okay, Mandy," I soothed her. "This is my
friend, Inspector Krisbaum."

They stood almost nose to nose as Krisbaum pushed
cookies back to the center of the plate, then licked his
finger. Mandy's chest heaved, as if it took all her courage to remain there.

"I wonder if I could ask you a quick question, Miss,
um . . . ?"

I spoke for Mandy, though it felt uncomfortably Edgar Bergen-ish. "McGuire. Mandy McGuire. If you
could back up, Inspector . . . she's a little phobic. The
inspector just wants to know if you remember what time
I got here tonight."

Mandy turned to me, searching my face for the right
answer.

"If you remember, please tell him."

"Five to seven," she stammered. "Five to seven."

Krisbaum tenderly placed the cookies on the coffee
table, between the two red-eyed panthers. "Did you
look at a clock?"

"Justin was waiting by the window. He told me. He
said she was early."

Krisbaum frowned. "Early for what?"

She looked bewildered. "Early. For when she usually
comes."

"All right. Would you mind asking Mr. Poat to come
in here for a minute, please?"

Mandy edged through the door, looking like she'd
been ordered to cross a mine field.

"Why is it so important, when I got home?"

Krisbaum grinned. "It's not, really."

"But you want another look at Poat?"

"It gives me a complex when people run away from me."

"It's someone in my office, isn't it? Someone else died, didn't they?" My voice was flat. All I felt was tired. Not even stoned. I didn't smoke to get stoned anymore. I'd been smoking so long it didn't alter my consciousness, it just made me feel kindlier toward it. "That's why I was hired, I guess."

Krisbaum understood what I was saying. "Bud Hopper, right? The big conspiracy?" He helped himself to a cookie before reclaiming the broken-down recliner. "Let me suggest an alternative, Miss Jansson. Say a person gets traumatized—badly traumatized—and say she fixes on somebody as a white knight type, you know, a hero that saves her from the gallows kind of thing. Well, say that hero just sees himself as a regular Joe doing his job—not necessarily some kind of Galahad. Well, he might want to go about his life, business as usual, you know, and forget all about her. And the damsel in distress (who's not in distress anymore), she might feel hurt by that. Neglected. She might even feel neglected enough to get herself back in distress just to get the white knight interested in her again."

"She'd have to be a moron," I observed.

"A fool for love," he said gently.

"Which I'm not."

Krisbaum raised the cookie to his mouth. "A modern lady might just hate to admit it to herself."

"Does the lieutenant believe this crap?"

Krisbaum sat there munching his cookie. He didn't seem inclined to answer. And since Justin Poat appeared in the doorway, I had to let it drop.

"Mr. Poat," Krisbaum said with a friendly smile. "Miss Jansson here will tell you she doesn't mind you answering a few questions about what time she got home tonight."

Poat looked pale and stiff. His lower lip was pulled away from his teeth, making him look cadaverous. "You haven't done enough to me?"

Krisbaum's eyes glinted with interest. "I don't think we've met before, have we?"

"Don't I pee in a cup for you every week?"

"Ah. On parole, are you?"

"I suppose you have a right to ask me anything you want." His voice was bitter, almost teary.

Poor bastard. "It's okay, Justin," I reassured him. "It's me he's interested in. Mandy said you saw me come home at five to seven. Is that—"

Krisbaum stood up, putting his big sloppy body between me and Poat. "That's right, Mr. Poat. You give up many privileges and rights as a parolee." He stepped closer to Poat, threateningly close. "And one of them is the luxury to tell a cop to go screw."

I stood too, looking around Krisbaum at Poat. Why was the inspector feeding the poor man's paranoia? "Justin—"

Krisbaum cast a glaring glance over his shoulder, silencing me. "You understand that?" he boomed.

Poat nodded grudgingly, his face a mask of suppressed fury.

"What were you in for?"

"Agg-aggravated assault."

"On who?"

"A bank officer where I w-worked."

"With what?"

"P-pipe."

"How do you know Miss Jansson?"

"My mother owns this—"

Krisbaum wheeled on me. "I'm talking to Poat." I took a hasty step away before Krisbaum turned back to Justin. "I want the truth. Not this obvious bullshit about her being your landlady's daughter!"

Poat's whole body went rigid. You could have ironed shirts on him, used him as a ramp.

Another step closer and Krisbaum had all but pinned him to the doorframe. "There's more to it than that, isn't there, Poat? In fact, I'm thinking maybe I should talk to your parole officer."

They stood there for a minute or two, Poat white and barely breathing, Krisbaum huffing and flushed. In the hall behind Poat, Mandy broke into sobs.

Finally Krisbaum backed away, barking to me, "Get your coat if you want it. We're going to the Hall."

28

I GOT ANOTHER dose of Krisbaum's theory in his car, which turned out to be a yacht-sized Buick with no shock absorbers. As we bumped through the Western Addition, he murmured that it was difficult sometimes to "re-achieve closeness." His sidelong glance invited me to pour out my heart to him.

Re-achieving Closeness Through Murder—it sounded like a self-help seminar by Leo Buscaglia and Charles

Manson. "It's not like getting my shoes reheeled because I have a crush on the shoe repairman," I sputtered.

"But the feeling is there," he said simply.

"No! I meant, for the sake of argument—"

"I'm not an idiot. You get in trouble, who do you call?"

"The cops! What's so strange about that?" I would have found it plenty strange, a couple of years ago.

"Not 'the cops'! A *particular* cop."

"Why are you dragging me to the Hall of Justice? What am I supposed to have done?" My voice was climbing to a screech.

"A colleague of yours is in the hospital, Miss Jansson."

"Melinda?" I felt weak and battered; almost wished I hadn't asked. "Melinda Karastatos?"

Krisbaum shouted at a bag lady who staggered off the curb in front of his car. We'd reached the Civic Center without my even noticing.

"Is she going to be okay?"

"Karastatos? Yeah, she's fine."

"What happened?"

Krisbaum made a show of concentrating on his driving. He didn't answer.

I closed my eyes. I could hear honking cars and boom boxes as we crossed Market Street. South of Market the sounds changed to mariachi music piped out of small restaurants and clanging metal from brick factories. I opened my eyes to see the two-tiered Embarcadero freeway rising like the Great Wall of China between the neighborhood and the waterfront. A stream of white headlights on the bottom tier and red taillights on the top made it look neon. We drove past some all-night bail bond and criminal law offices, into an underground parking garage labeled AUTHORIZED PER-

SONNEL ONLY. The Hall of Justice was becoming as familiar to me as a favorite shopping spot.

I found myself lamenting, "It's not my fault!"

Krisbaum turned off the engine and cut his headlights. It was glaringly bright down there without them. "What's not your fault?"

I twisted in my seat to face him. "It's not my fault that I've been here so many times! That these things keep happening!"

His face looked lavender in the winking fluorescence. "Whose fault is it?" he asked quietly.

"You know I didn't kill anybody in law school. You know I didn't kill Julian Warneke. And now—" My mouth was dry, my eyes itched, my neck and shoulders ached. It wasn't fair. I should be home in my own apartment, smoking pot and soaking in a tub full of suds. "I was framed!"

Krisbaum smiled wryly. I guess he'd heard that before. "You're not under arrest, you know."

"Just being back here—!"

"We've been fair with you," he objected. "We treat you with respect, don't we?"

"My dentist treats me with respect. That doesn't mean I want to see him every night!"

"Would you feel better if I told you the lieutenant wanted to talk to you?" He smiled soothingly.

It took an effort of will not to slap him. "You patronizing son of a bitch!"

That wiped the smile off his face. "I don't like that kind of talk from scum off the street, and I like it even less from a lady lawyer!"

"Lady *lawyer*? What's *that* got to do with anything?"

"A lot!" He slapped the steering wheel. "We've been extra careful with you guys, believe me. But this is the limit! If I have to stop respecting your rights to keep people from getting poisoned, then by gosh I will! If I have to start pushing you around, then I'll push!"

"Me? Me personally?"

But Krisbaum was climbing out of the car. A moment later he flung open the passenger door and waited glumly for me to get out. We rode the police elevator without speaking.

His comments had been general, I told myself. He was mad at lawyers; half the people I met were.

I glanced at him. He was scowling at the elevator door. He certainly looked willing to push me around. Me personally.

Oh well, as long as Melinda was all right. Some nerve I had feeling sorry for myself when she was in the hospital.

We got out at the fourth floor, Room 450, Homicide Detail. It was a not-big-enough, well-lighted room with perhaps twenty desks pushed into pairs, some back to back, some side by side. There were file folders and papers everywhere, and a number of portly ex-jocks talking on the phone or filling out forms. The room smelled of cheap coffee, sweat and cigarette smoke. One corner was partitioned off with glass walls and miniblinds. The blinds weren't quite closed. I could see the lieutenant in there, standing behind his desk with his suit jacket buttoned and his tie neatly tacked. Opposite him, a man balanced a minicam on his shoulder.

Krisbaum took my elbow and maneuvered me through the maze of desks and men, past a wall taped with Larson cartoons and into a room barely big enough for a wooden table and four sturdy chairs. "Wait here," he commanded.

The cubicle was windowless and unornamented. There was nothing to look at except flaws in the white cork walls. An air conditioner blew quietly. It was like an office elevator with a table in it.

But it had associations. I'd once spent most of a night here, under arrest and spilling my guts. Able to keep my mother's criminal activity secret because the lieutenant had agreed in advance that I could. He'd ended up shooting someone, to insure the secret got kept. It had been that important to him to get me to tell the truth. To exculpate me.

"And if that's not love, what is?" I quoted the old song.

Unfortunately, Krisbaum chose that moment to fling open the door. He stood in the doorway, looking like he'd just seen the burning bush. Through the open door came the sound of ringing phones and a bark of male laughter. He closed the door and sat beside me, carefully setting a small tape recorder on the table in front of us.

I scraped my chair back toward the wall, wondering why he didn't sit across the table from me, as usual.

"Before I turn this thing on, I want to tell you something. I've talked to the lieutenant. He's agreed to limit his involvement in this case. Administration only. Which," he added, "is supposed to be what he does in every case, instead of getting involved in the investigation."

He didn't allow me time to comment. He clicked on the tape recorder. "Your name is Willa June Jansson and I am San Francisco Police Inspector Daniel Krisbaum. I'm going to ask you some questions, but first I want to ask you whether you've been mistreated by me in any way."

"No," I murmured.

"Did I coerce you into agreeing to answer questions for me?"

"No."

"Are you cooperating with this investigation of your own free will?"

Free will. I considered getting existential: *What is free will?* "Yes."

"Please describe your movements today from the

time you woke up to right now." He checked his watch. "Ten oh seven."

"I went to my office this morning at around seven, and"—Krisbaum interrupted to get the firm's name and address on record—"I picked up some documents, then I—"

"Who did you see when you were at your office?"

"Nobody. It was too early; the receptionist"—Krisbaum's partner, Kelly—"and the secretaries weren't in yet. Melinda Karastatos was in her office, I think, but her door was closed. I didn't talk to her." I'd been afraid to. Afraid she resented Mott's last minute substitution in the Malhousie case. "I went to my office and got the documents I needed and looked them over for a while, then went back out."

"You didn't go into any other offices?"

"Most of them are empty right now. It's just me and Melinda and William Mott."

"You didn't go into William Mott's office?"

"No. He wasn't in. His door was open. The lights were off."

"You saw his door open."

"Yes." I knew better than to try to hurry one of these interrogations. I waited.

"Did you step inside his office?"

"Of course not. Why should I?"

"In the course of business, what reason would you have for going into Mott's office?"

I blinked at him. The bright light made his skin look matte and grainy. Where the hell was this going? "Conference. Pick up or drop off documents. I don't know. It's a business. Business reasons. All kinds of them."

"You didn't go in there this morning. For 'business reasons'?"

"No." I was replaying our conversation in the car. He'd said a colleague of mine was in the hospital. I'd asked if it was Melinda, if she was all right. And he'd said Melinda was fine. But he hadn't said *she* was the one in the hospital. "Oh, my god. Is it Bill Mott? Is Mott the one who's in the hospital?"

Krisbaum sighed and scratched his belly, apparently giving the question some thought. Then he said, "William K. Mott just died, Miss Jansson. From poison hemlock he ingested some time during the workday. Now, if you could just tell us—"

But he had to ask the next question several times. He had to give me an impatient tap on the arm, in fact, before I answered, "No, I didn't go into the attorney's lounge. I didn't put anything into the refrigerator."

Bob LeVoq and now William Mott. My bosses. Both killed the way my last boss was killed. Killed like Julian Warneke. "Bud Hopper—"

"Don't!" Krisbaum gripped my shoulders. "I don't want to hear about this Hopper character again!"

"But can't you see why the killer's using hemlock? It's because Julian—"

He shook me. Not quite hard enough to give me whiplash; hard enough to tell me he'd push me around if he had to. "I said no more conspiracy bullshit! We're talking about *you*." He clicked off the tape recorder. "We're talking about something that happened between you and Don Surgelato a few months ago. We're going to get real tonight. Understand?"

I guess I didn't look like I did. He shook me again. Harder. "The Civil Service Commission orders a homicide investigation whenever a cop kills a suspect, did you know that, Miss Jansson?" There was frustration in his voice, maybe even pain. "Me and Kelly investigated the lieutenant. And we gave him a clean bill of health, sure. But I'm not stupid. There was a piece missing from his story, and you're it."

"No."

"I came to Homicide when I was twenty-six years old. When Don was still kicking around a pigskin. And

I don't turn a blind eye. Not even to protect a friend. I want you to be clear on that!"

"Take your hands off me."

There was a cynical glint in his eye as he complied. Then, deliberately, he turned the tape recorder back on.

Just as deliberately, I spoke the forbidden name. "Bud Hopper."

29

"**E**ARTH WOMAN! You look terrible!" My landlord reached instinctively for my arm, though I had no intention of swooning.

I brushed his liver-spotted hand away. "I don't have my keys. Let me into my apartment, will you?"

He disappeared momentarily into what he called Spaceship A, then came back into the hall with the key to (what I called) Apartment B. "Where have you been?"

"For the last four and a half hours, at the Hall of Justice. I'm glad you're still up. My purse is at Mother's

Fresh Start Commune, and I don't feel like facing the Addams Family right now.''

He tapped the key against my keyhole a few times, squinting shortsightedly. I took it away and unlocked my door. Unaired for three days, the apartment smelled like a laundry hamper. It looked like one, too. If I still had a job, maybe I'd hire a cleaning lady. ''I knew it couldn't last!'' I lamented.

''Troubles?'' He sounded vaguely hopeful. He and my parents didn't want me to keep the job. They didn't want me to take a respite from the cannibalism of left-wing politics. They didn't want me to earn a decent wage.

I couldn't keep anger out of my voice. ''Everything's peachy. Except that my boss just got poisoned. My other boss. That makes three. I'm two ahead of Plato, now.''

He stuck his neck forward and tilted his head. With his long yellow-white hair and leathery face, he resembled an aging orangutan.

I stepped closer. ''You know what else? Those two cornflakes Mother installed at Julian's house are nothing but trouble! They're going to burn the place down, or kill each other or something! What's *wrong* with you guys?''

I slammed into the bathroom to run a tub of hot water. Whatever was wrong with them, I was stuck with them now. I'd never get a decent law job again. It would take all my left-wing connections (the only kind I had, alas) to get into a shoestring Legal Aid clone. I'd be back to busboy wages and the same old crap. Visualize peace and pass the 1985 Napa Valley Chardonnay (''You can't go wrong with an '85 Chardonnay, comrade!'').

My phone was ringing, so I went out to the living room and took it off the hook. Then I smoked a joint and soaked in the tub. My briefcase and suits were at the commune, but it probably didn't make any difference. The office would be closed until the cops were through searching for traces of the hemlock that killed Mott. Unless he'd been poisoned while dining alone at Jack's (where Krisbaum said he'd eaten lunch), then he'd gotten the dose from something in the attorneys' lounge refrigerator. Or from someone who'd come to see him that day (Krisbaum would not elaborate).

Anyway, the San Francisco office of Wailes, Roth was probably "somewhat defunct," in the words of the New York partner who'd initially contacted me. Thomas Spender (I think his name was) might even think it was completely defunct.

The work was dull and the hours long, but I was feeling sentimental about the job when I crawled into bed that night. I found myself persuaded by the lie I'd told my mother. Women (me in particular) *should* make good money and wield power. I was thirty-five years old; it had taken me a long time to "buy the myth" (as the Trotskyites used to say), but I'd done it with a convert's passion. I *wanted* ninety thousand a year. I *wanted* Mercedes dealers to quake in fear when I bared my mighty writs.

I woke up feeling the same way. So I was distressed to hear Melinda Karastatos say California Bank & Trust had "withdrawn its custom."

She was crammed into the narrow director's chair next to my bookcase. On the floor beside her foot, had she been in a noticing mood, was an ashtray full of marijuana roaches. It was barely eight o'clock. I was still in my sweat clothes. Melinda, with no particular place to go, wore a gray pinstripe suit, pearl nylons and black pumps. Her eyes were red-rimmed and her hair drooped into a poor imitation of its usual pageboy. She'd been up most of the night, she said. Frowning at her big hands, she added, "Working. On a CBT matter, in fact. And then Tom Spender phones me at home. From New York. Five o'clock in the morning, our time. He doesn't care about the time difference. He never did."

She scowled; I could see it was more than the time difference. It was the lack of respect Spencer displayed in ignoring it. "He called to say Villa-Fuentes wants all CBT's files sent to Colin Aasgar! Aasgar! That *snake*!" She added bitterly, "Aasgar certainly ended up with everything he wanted! And without that lazy LeVoq as his baggage!"

I wondered if it was an observation or an accusation. I also wondered if I should mention William Mott. She hadn't so far, but that didn't fool me into thinking she didn't care. If her pale face and red eyes were any indication, she cared more than she could comfortably express. I knew the feeling well. It had been hell talking about Julian after he died. I still resented one particular conversation with my mother: she'd accused me of not esteeming Julian just because I wouldn't cry in public. I wasn't going to make that mistake with Melinda.

"Melinda?" I was seated on the scarred coffee table, maybe five feet away from her. She stared at her lap. I could see a glimmer of tears under her pale lashes. "Are we still in business?"

She kept her eyes open, not blinking. If there were tears there, she was determined not to shed them. Thank god. "No. There's no San Francisco office, as of this morning. Spender wants to 'disassociate the firm from the tragedy.' " Her unconscious mimicry gave the words a staccato New Yawrk sound.

I let my spine curl, glancing at the ashtray full of roaches. I supposed it was too early in the morning to get stoned. But then again, I didn't have any place to go. So much for my big break.

When I looked at Melinda again, she was looking at me. Her eyes were bloodshot, her skin flushed. "My partnership vote is next week. *Next week!* I've put years into this firm! I brought in most of our clients, and watched that son of a bitch LeVoq take credit for it! And now, days before my vote, they pull the office out

from under me!'' She scowled at something behind me.
''I'll live in L.A. if I have to, but Wailes, Roth owes
me this partnership! I've earned it!''

She wasn't the only one feeling sorry for herself. ''I
made twenty-five five working for Julian. With fifty
thousand in student loans to repay.'' I guessed I didn't
have to add, What the hell am I supposed to do now?

She leaned forward in the director's chair, making the
legs splay slightly. A big woman. Even Daddy didn't
make the chair creak. ''Come with me!''

''Where?''

The gleam was back in her eyes. But not tears, this
time. Determination? Obsession?

''Los Angeles. Right now. This morning. To lobby
for our jobs.''

''But you said the office was—''

''The *San Francisco* office!''

''You mean—Work in *L.A.*?'' That endless sprawl of
pink stucco and brown air?

''They owe us, Willa! They can't expect us to bear
the brunt of this—this—!''

''Imbroglio?''

''What are we supposed to say to interviewers from
other firms? That we were laid off because our boss
was—'' She clamped her lips shut. Realizing, I think,
that I'd had this problem before.

''If I worked in L.A.—'' I was struck by the acumen
of her plan. ''I could quit after a while, and not have
to tell interviewers it was because of—''

She nodded.

''And if you were a partner down there, you could
lateral into a San Francisco firm, eventually.''

''Yes!'' There was an explosion of feeling in that
word: loathing for L.A., love of San Francisco. Other
stuff I couldn't identify.

''Leave San Francisco.'' I'd looked down my nose at
them, in law school; scrambling for big bucks and not

caring where they had to go to get them. Houston, L.A., Philadelphia. Jesus, even Buffalo.

" 'Disassociate the firm from the tragedy.' " Again, she quoted Spender bitterly. "What he's saying is, cut us adrift. A couple of months' severance pay and the hell with you. The hell with your career. The hell with years of carrying the office on your shoulders and not getting any credit for it!"

Leave San Francisco. My family.

I was surprised to feel a stirring of relief. My parents and their damn causes, moralizing at me, disapproving of everything from my job to my "bad relationship" with pot. Turning Julian's beautiful house into the Bates Motel. I'd told my landlord the truth: I was sick of my parents' bullshit.

Sick of Surgelato's bullshit, too. For a minute, in the back of an unmarked police car, I thought we'd reached a kind of understanding. Now I posed a threat to his career. Our understanding had cost him, and he resented me for it.

I felt tears sting my eyes. Why stick around here? Nothing was going right.

The only thing I had going for me was my job. It wasn't fun, but it was a chance to dig myself out of a financial hole. Pay back loans. Buy a little comfort; I'd been relying too heavily on the green and leafy kind. A couch would be nice. A television. Dinners out. Cab fare to plays.

"When do we leave?"

30

MELINDA DROVE THE rented car through the miles and miles of "valley" between LAX and downtown. On either side of us, one-story buildings squatted in a yellow haze. Here and there, oleander or hibiscus or jacaranda exploded in candy-colored blooms, dwarfing the drab structures. Utility wires stretched across every street. On every corner, billboards displayed smiling smokers or sunbathers or scotch drinkers.

By the time we reached downtown, I was having qualms. Four square blocks of monoliths. No colorful little shops, no flower vendors, no town square. Just blank facades and traffic, endless rushing traffic. Hotels with shopping malls inside them.

I looked out the passenger window and thought, *What the hell am I doing here?*

Unfortunately, the Los Angeles law partners had much the same reaction.

Jonathan Seeder greeted us with affronted formality.

"Melinda, Willa. You should have told us you were

coming so we could reserve rooms for you." Talk you out of it, he really meant.

I'd spent half an hour with Melinda in the airport bathroom, watching her wield a curling iron, mascara wand and makeup brush. It was the first time I'd ever seen her in makeup. Orange-smeared cheeks and gooey eyelids didn't make her look any better, but she did look more L.A. She'd even exchanged the pinstriped suit for a cream silk, which she wore with a gray shirt and heels.

"Given the situation, we thought it best to discuss the matter in person." She took the stiffness out of her words with a lip-glossed smile.

Seeder, wearing his stop-sign red vest under a taupe suit, smoothed back his thinning waves. We were in a ballroom-sized conference room, seated at one end of a table so vast it had to be installed while the building was under construction (or so Sean Kowalski had bragged). Floor-to-ceiling glass walls revealed L.A. at twilight, lights blinking through streaks of brown smog.

Seeder smiled at Melinda, his eyes cold and un-friendly. I remembered my interview dinner, Seeder's enthusiastic praise of LeVoq the "rainmaker." The bat-tle line had long been drawn: LeVoq on one side, Me-linda on the other. LeVoq's death hadn't shifted Seeder's allegiance.

His tone wistful and his smile chiseled in stone, he began justifying New York's "quick amputation" of the San Francisco office.

Melinda interrupted. "Yes, we understand their rea-soning. But it's one thing to abandon a sinking ship and another thing entirely to let your crew go down with it. It'll create a major scandal if you don't transfer us down to this office, Jon. The legal community will assume you suspect us of—" She licked her waxy lips and blinked a few times. Overcome, perhaps. Or waiting

for Seeder to express a confidence in us he probably
didn't feel.

"You know we don't blame you for any of the unfortunate . . . incidents." He traced a black vein in the
marble tabletop. "We were discussing it this morning,
and in our view, you two are victims just as surely
as—" He caught himself before speaking their names.
"As surely as the office itself."

Melinda touched her reddened cheeks, as if suddenly
embarrassed by them. "The point is, the firm can't afford to be perceived as the kind of employer that turns
its back on its own people. That cuts line when they're
in trouble."

The stony smile was cracking. "We assumed you'd
want to remain in San Francisco, but we are quite prepared to be generous with severance—"

"If we stay in San Francisco, the legal community
will interpret it as a lack of confidence. On your part
for not transferring us—or more likely on our part, for
not sticking with the firm after all the bad publicity it's
gotten. Especially after that *American Lawyer* article."
Melinda waited for this point to register on Seeder's
plump face. Then she added, "Wailes, Roth can't afford to lose any more attorneys right now, Jon. Willa
and I came here to tell you we're willing to uproot
ourselves and move to Los Angeles as a public expression of our loyalty to the firm."

Seeder glanced at me, obviously dismayed. And I
said valiantly, "I'd feel guilty about remaining in San
Francisco!"

31

MELINDA DISAPPEARED INTO the belly of the beast, and I got snared by Sean Kowalski.

He was murmuring about moonlight in Malibu, bright lights and night stars and the glamor that fades by day. He leaned a meaty arm on the wall in front of me. Trapped against the burlap wallpaper, I wondered why I didn't find him attractive. In my entire life, I'd never fallen for a conventionally handsome man.

"Did you ever talk to someone called Bud Hopper?" Hopper was on my mind, and since there was no polite way to duck under Kowalski's arm, I thought I might as well ask.

Kowalski's leer faded. He pushed himself off the wall and took a backward step. "You were asking about Hopper at the Mariposa retreat."

"He got me this job, but I haven't met anybody yet who's actually talked to him." I ran my fingers through my hair. Kowalski's expression told me he'd never do that to his own curls.

119

"I thought—" He showed a slight flush under his golden brows. "Didn't William Mott . . ."

"No. At least, he told me he'd never talked to Hopper himself."

"I don't know. I just heard Mott went to bat for you . . . after Bob . . ."

I think Kowalski expected a grateful eulogy. He looked a little disgusted when I climbed right back on my hobbyhorse. "Did he use Hopper's recommendation as a reason the firm should keep me on?"

Kowalski was looking up and down the hall, ready to attach himself to the first woman who showed her face. "I think that might have been part of it."

"But he told me he didn't talk to Hopper himself. It must have been someone down here. Possibly senior to him. Someone whose judgment he trusted." Milward Kael?

Kowalski was getting the glazed look people get when they talk to cranks. It made me want to explain my reasoning.

"He wouldn't have put much faith in Hopper's recommendation if it had been relayed to him by the janitor. See? He heard it once from Thomas Spender, when I got hired. But later, before the retreat—"

Kowalski was edging away, smiling toothily. "Well, give me a call next time you're down, Willa. We'll do the Pacific Coast Highway."

For lack of a better plan, I made my way to the attorneys' lounge (where, sure enough, both cross-country ski machines were in use). Conversation ceased when I entered. Curious eyes inspected my San Francisco wool and my unmoussed hair.

The woman I'd met at my interview dinner patted a cushion on the white leather couch, saying, "You're just in time for happy hour." From behind a Japanese screen came the tinkle of ice being dropped into glasses. "I heard you're planning to transfer down to this office?"

Opposite us on wing chairs, a cherubic young man and a stylishly desiccated older woman exchanged glances.

"Yes." I was facing a wall of windows. I could see little lighted rectangles in rectangular buildings. Not like San Francisco, where the hills present waves of odd night shapes and crowded lights. "I hope so."

A uniformed man, handsome enough to host a talk show, brought out a tray of margaritas and Perriers. I took a margarita. It tasted like salty peroxide.

"We've had the police here," the woman said tentatively. "We're awfully sorry. If there's anything we can do. We know Melinda must be . . ." She shook her head.

I put the drink down on a small block of marble. "She's being very professional. That's probably the best way to handle it."

The young man rose from his wing chair and joined the two lounge skiers. They looked funny as hell, their designer-suited limbs sliding back and forth on rail-bound skis. The older woman said, "I'm Kathy Sim."

"Willa Jansson."

She nodded curtly. She knew who I was, all right.

"You'll have to pardon Carey," the younger woman said quietly. "He found out today he didn't make partner."

"This office is so damn top-heavy," the older woman complained. "Fifty-four percent partners. I wonder if any of us will make it, when the time comes."

The younger woman raised her brows and nodded thoughtfully. "Carey's leaving. No use being a permanent drone!"

"They should have warned him last year! After the straw vote!"

I thought of Melinda. "I was told they were voting next week."

"They moved it up because of the golf tournament."

"Did they vote on . . . everyone?"

The woman nodded grimly. The eyes beneath the blue-dusted lids told me what I wanted to know.

"Nobody made partner this year?"

"Nobody," she confirmed.

I picked up my margarita. It wasn't pot but it was better than nothing.

I had two more before I staggered out of there.

Melinda was still closeted with Jonathan Seeder and Milward Kael when a lounge skier directed me down the street to the Bonaventure. The firm, he told me, always lodged its visiting attorneys there.

32

THE SUITE WAS bigger than my apartment. It had two televisions, a Jacuzzi tub, a bar, and a minirefrigerator full of designer chocolate. I was flopped out on the king-sized bed watching Sylvester Stallone recapture Vietnam. I'd made short business of my room service tray, and smoked one of the two joints I'd brought with me. I wasn't letting myself think about William Mott or Bob LeVoq or even Julian Warneke, and I was feeling all right, considering.

. It didn't last long.

Someone pounded on my door. I clicked off the TV and found Melinda in the hallway, apparently about to beat the door down. Her curling-ironed bangs did a limp parody of L.A. hair, her silk suit was crumpled, and her experiment with makeup had smudged. More noticeably, she looked furious. Her nostrils were white, there were painful-looking red furrows between her brows, and her shoulders were drawn up to her ears. I took an involuntary step backward.

"I'm going to the police!" she said through clenched teeth. "And to *hell* with them! I *carried* that office! LeVoq was a lazy, obnoxious jerk and Aasgar shoved everything on the baby lawyers—leaving *me* to supervise them! A *rainmaker*! This firm doesn't need a rainmaker! It doesn't need someone to bring clients *in*—it needs someone to *keep* the clients we've got! It needs someone to do the damn work and win the damn cases! How long do they think CBT would have stayed with us if we hadn't won their motions?" Her head trembled furiously on its short neck. "Permanent associate! That's the reward I get! Well—They've got one more chance! That's it! I told them: next week. Next week, I come down to L.A. as a partner, or I go to *The American Lawyer* with some *real* news!"

A couple in matching velour jogging suits got off the elevator and started toward us, carrying parcels from the hotel's tri-level mall. I tried to draw Melinda into the room.

She shook off my arm. "Our flight leaves at eight in the morning. I just called the SFPD. They said it's okay to go back into the office. I want to get our files sorted and shipped down here. I want to get packed and out of there!"

Momentarily, her anger gave way to a grimace of pain. Had she really loved that old Republican?

She wheeled around, almost colliding with the velour couple, and stalked down the hall.

I closed and bolted my door, turned the TV back on and smoked the other joint. At eleven o'clock, the L.A. news ran a feature on William Mott. Yale Law class of '56, clerk for Supreme Court Justice Frankfurter, five years with the Justice Department and twenty more with Wailes, Roth. He'd been on the verge of nomination for a federal court judgeship.

Suddenly, a trench-coated young woman appeared on the TV screen, one hand gripping a microphone, the other anchoring wind-whipped hair off her face. She was standing in front of my apartment building. "In what *may* be no more than a bizarre coincidence," the woman informed the camera, "attorney Willa Jansson, previously a suspect in two other serial murder cases, is—" I muted the sound. Thank god for remote control.

I stood up, walking closer to the screen. There it was, all right: home. A weatherbeaten little rowhouse on a street festooned with streetcar wires. Seeing it on television, without benefit of that now-I-can-relax feeling, I realized how drab it was. Maybe I wouldn't miss it.

One thing for sure, I wasn't going back to it tomorrow, not if out-of-town newscasters were lurking there. I could stand Justin and Mandy a few more days.

33

I *THOUGHT* I could stand Charlie and Squeaky a few more days. That was before they greeted me as a beloved prodigal.

Justin opened the door, gaped at me, then caught me in an embrace that needed only a comradely bussing of cheeks. An instant later he released me, saying, "The cops were here asking about you, but I didn't tell them anything!" His tone implied that they'd ground out cigarettes on his arm.

I stepped past him, kicking my Macy's bag into the hall. "It's okay to talk to the police about me. They just want to—"

"Mandy!" Justin cut me off with an excited shout. "Mandy! She's back!"

And suddenly Mandy flew out of the kitchen, her arms extended and her caftan sleeves billowing. She too embraced me, but unlike Justin, she clung to me, breaking into sobs.

It would have been mean-spirited to push her away,

but I wanted to. So I'd spent a couple of nights else-where; so what? Where did Mother find these people?

Finally Mandy released me, mopping tears off her horsey face with a caftan sleeve. "Are they going to *arrest* you?" There was more panic in her words than even I, potential arrestee, felt.

"How long were you in the San Bruno Jail, Mandy?"

Her face crumpled and her chest heaved a few times before she replied, "Twenty-seven months."

I'd been there two months. Two months of claustro-phobic madness. Of crying every night. Of living for my weekly visiting hour and feeling crushed by grief when it was over.

Twenty-seven months. No wonder.

"They're not going to arrest me, Mandy, honest. I didn't do anything they can arrest me for."

Mandy didn't look convinced, but she struggled to act cheerful. "I made some dinner," she warbled.

I feigned enthusiasm. "Oh, good!"

It was either brisket of radial tire or pot roast. Justin, a kinder person than I, had seconds. I told Mandy I was on a diet, and she said she'd save a piece for my lunch.

I toyed with the idea of calling Krisbaum and telling him I was back. But I didn't need another lecture on the Manson Method of Achieving Closeness. It could wait until morning.

34

ANDREW MCNEE STOOD at the receptionist's desk stuffing wilted flower arrangements into garbage sacks. "I've been keeping the cards and sending new flowers to the hospital," he said dryly, pointing to a pile of florist cards beside the telephone. "Most of them are for Mr. Mott. A few late ones for Mr. LeVoq. I also arranged to have our calls ring directly through to the answering service. I assume Ms. Karastatos will want to phone each client personally—in her own time."

I nodded, a little overwhelmed. McNee—or possibly Krisbaum—had requested that a guard be posted in the corridor separating our suite of offices from the rest of the twentieth floor. Thanks to our Cerberus in blue, the office was nearly empty. Just McNee canceling court dates, Rhonda copying files, and Melinda and I sorting them into boxes marked L.A./TO STORE, L.A./OPEN FILES, or SHIP TO LAW OFFICE OF C. AASGAR. A moving company was coming later to pack law books and office supplies. We didn't say much to each other beyond what was necessary to the task.

At two o'clock, Melinda brought out a big plaid thermos and a stack of Styrofoam cups. She handed us each a cup and poured out three strong, spicy Bloody Marys. Then she poured herself one and set the thermos on McNee's desk. The four of us guzzled the drinks in silence; no one proposed a toast. As soon as we were through, Melinda handed McNee and Rhonda each an envelope. Four months' pay, she explained solemnly. Plus a small bonus. Rhonda burst into tears, and McNee, obviously impatient with his assistant, hustled her out of the office.

"Go ahead and clean out your desk," Melinda said calmly. She wore gray wool slacks and a white cotton shirt: probably as close to sloppy as she ever got. Her eyes were red and she occasionally blew her nose, pointedly mentioning an allergy to dust. "I'll be in Bill's office, packing his things to send down to L.A. LeVoq's wife will be in later to pick up his personal items." She frowned. "If you could keep her away from me, I'd appreciate it." She walked quickly out of the reception area.

I sat on McNee's desk, idly screwing the plastic cup back on Melinda's thermos. I could still taste the tabasco-laden drink. I considered having another; maybe it would reconcile me to my decision. Four months pay and a bonus, the firm had given McNee. At my salary, that would be over thirty thousand dollars. Twenty thousand, net, just for walking away now. More than I'd cleared in a year, working for Julian Warneke. I could make Jonathan Seeder happy, and I wouldn't have to live in L.A. I could go away somewhere—Jamaica, maybe—until this whole murder thing blew over.

Sure I could. And never get another decent law job again.

My bubble pricked, I wandered into the attorneys'
lounge. Alas, no handsome waiter—just a refrigerator.
I opened it looking for something to eat, but found only
the sandwich Mandy had prepared for me from last
night's Michelin. The cops had stripped the refrigerator
bare, leaving only a few smears of gray fingerprint
powder.

I stood at the lounge window, looking at cold blue
sky and scurrying wisps of cloud, at Coit Tower, small
and quaint on a distant hill. Twenty floors below me,
the street flowed with gray and navy suits, with splashes
of designer colors. Balloon bouquets fluttered over
flower stands, and a tuxedoed string quartet staked out
a bit of plaza.

I didn't have the heart to go out for lunch, to walk
the bustling streets. It was hard enough, saying good-
bye to San Francisco. Mandy's sandwich was awful, but
I stood there eating it.

I heard Melinda's voice behind me, summing up my
thoughts: "Why did it have to happen?"

I turned to her, noticing she carried the thermos jug
of Bloody Marys. Mandy's sandwich was stuck in my
throat. "Is there any left?"

Frowning, she poured the remainder into the plastic
thermos lid and handed it to me. "It was hard out there,
with Rhonda and Andrew. What was I supposed to say?
Cheers? To absent friends?"

The dregs were even worse than my first sample. Almost as bad as Mandy's sandwich. "Have you eaten?"

She put the thermos in the lounge's small sink. "I've
got what I spiked the Marys with. I plan to drink my
lunch today."

I considered asking her for a shot of vodka (or whatever goes into a Bloody Mary to make it taste so me-
dicinal). It had to be better than what I was drinking.
The tabasco had settled to the bottom.

"LeVoq's wife is here. I went out to the reception

room and there she was. Sniffing the thermos." Melinda sighed deeply. "I offered her a drink, but she's not feeling very convivial, I guess." She scowled at the sink. "If she has any questions or problems, fob her off, will you? As far as I'm concerned, she can take anything she wants out of LeVoq's office, including the light bulbs."

"Okay."

We looked at one another. "I don't know which way they'll jump on making me partner," she said woodenly. "And I won't go down there as an associate."

I swallowed more of the tabascoey drink. Did she want a show of solidarity? Want me to say I wouldn't go without her?

I could feel myself flush. My shirt was sticking to my back. Maybe Melinda's résumé could survive a connection with one "imbroglio"; mine couldn't survive three. For me, it was L.A. or nothing. Nothing I wanted; nothing I could live on.

She looked at me searchingly. I rubbed my knuckles over my lips. They were tingling.

She backed up, groping for the door. "All my years here. Building up a client base. Keeping CBT happy. L.A. happy. Doing all Bob's work. Most of Colin's." She winced, holding up her hand as if the room had grown too bright. "It still came down around me."

"You did what you could," I offered feebly.

She closed her eyes and turned away, sliding through the partially open door.

Did what you could. A galling epitaph if there ever was one.

I rinsed out Melinda's thermos cup and filled it with water. My mouth felt blistered and my throat burned. My stomach churned with Mandy's home cooking. My eyes were beginning to tear. It would be just my luck to get sick on top of everything else.

I walked through the reception room, pausing in the

corridor between LeVoq's office and Mott's. What were the two women doing in their loved ones' offices? Were they crying? LeVoq's wife was half a million dollars richer with insurance proceeds; did that compensate for a philandering (if cheerfully charming) husband? William Mott had been no Lochinvar, but he'd been important to Melinda's career, if not her happiness.

Everywhere I go, people end up sad.

I leaned against the wall, massaging my throat. I felt like I'd just bitten into a jalapeño. My mouth and eyes were watering. I didn't feel able to talk.

And Bob LeVoq's wife chose that moment to come out of his office, toting a leather bag.

I was struck once again by how frothily pretty she was. Midtwenties, gold curls, complexion like a Christmas tree angel. She looked harassed, but not particularly sad. She let out a startled squeak when she heard me clear my throat. The leather tote slid off her shoulder to the floor.

She looked down at it, aghast. "Oh no," she murmured, dropping to a squat. She reached trembling fingers into the bag, pulling out several framed photographs separated by file folders. She flipped through them, gnawing her lower lip. "Bob's pictures of the kids," she said tightly. "I want to save them. When they grow up and have offices of their own—" She blinked up at me, a cloud of doubt in her eyes. People don't display their own baby pictures. She obviously hadn't thought it through.

I extended a hand to help her up. When she took it, I almost went down with her. I took a few dizzy breaths, leaning against McNee's desk.

She didn't seem to notice. She said, "Bob always had time for the kids. A lot of lawyers work weekends, but Bob always had time to give them swimming lessons. He got one of those bicycle cabooses and took them for bike rides." She managed a smile. "He made time for

the kids.'' Time he could have been helping Melinda
with his caseload. ''He took time to smell the flowers.''

And distribute them among the ladies. But I supposed
good fathers were rarer than faithful husbands.

She glanced at the door to Bill Mott's office. ''Bob
used to call Melinda a drone. He said diligence was
useless without creativity. That turtles only win the race
in fairy tales.''

She looked at me so intently that I wondered if she
were trying to tell me something.

''Bob used to say, slow and steady *loses* the race.''
His widow repeated the words as if they contained a
coded message. ''He said steady is another word for
dull, and the least you can be these days is *fast*. He told
the kids that, too.''

Again she looked at William Mott's office door.
''Melinda didn't win the race, did she?''

She hoisted her bag back onto her shoulder and
added, ''It was nice to talk to you again.''

I wiped a film of moisture off my cheeks. Why was
the office so warm? ''Thank you. Take care of yourself.''

I watched her leave, then I straggled to my office. I
sat heavily in my leather chair, turning it so I could
look out the window. Homogeneity and smog, that's
what I'd see from my window in L.A. Well, better that
than a windowless cubby in some shoestring firm; better that than a two-thirds cut in pay.

I patted the soft leather of my armrest, vowing, ''As
God is my witness, I'll never sit in vinyl again!''

''Oh, let's hope not!'' said a wry voice behind me.

I swiveled in my chair. ''Inspector Kris—!'' I swallowed several times. What was wrong with my throat?

''Did you hear I was looking for you?'' Krisbaum
was his usual elegant self in a blue suit and striped
apricot shirt.

''Yes. You scared Mandy half to death. She's still

very traumatized—'' I swallowed again, mopping my eyes and cheeks with my shirtsleeve.

Krisbaum was about to say something snide, I could tell by the clucking sound he made. But I was feeling too awful to maintain eye contact. I pressed the heels of my hands to my sinuses. They felt swollen, like a sudden head cold; worse, though—almost scalded.

''Hey!'' Krisbaum's voice was sharp. ''What the hell's wrong?''

He knelt beside my chair, pulling my hands off my face. My eyes were streaming. ''What's the matter?'' He sounded angry.

I shook my head. ''I feel—I don't know. Fluish. Like I've been eating hot peppers.''

''Oh, Christ! Come on!'' He grabbed my arm and stood up, yanking me up too. ''Come on! Hurry! If you can run, do it!''

''Run? I can run.'' But when I tried to walk, I doubled over. It felt like someone had taken a torch to my belly.

Krisbaum unceremoniously picked me up and staggered through the office with me. When we got to the end of the hall, he ordered everyone off the elevator and expressed us down to the basement.

Like a lot of huge office buildings, this one had a tiny infirmary near the security offices.

The first thing Krisbaum said to the woman in nurse's white was, ''Pump her stomach!'' He deposited me on a padded, paper-covered gurney.

The woman stood up, a Danielle Steel book sliding off her lap. ''What—? I'm supposed to ask—What—?''

He flashed his picture ID. ''Right *now!* If you don't know how to do it, then give me the equipment!''

''I know how,'' she said meekly, opening a cupboard and pulling out the most awful-looking contraption I've ever seen.

''Give her charcoal when you're done! Lots of it.

And *don't* dispose of the stomach contents! Where's your phone? We're going to need an ambulance!''

35

IT WAS HEMLOCK. And I was in the hospital for observation, which meant cheerful middle-aged women came in every hour or so and filled syringes with my blood. I suppose there must have been doctors in the hospital somewhere, but I never caught a glimpse of one. It was probably better that way; a glimpse of doctor can be prohibitively expensive. (At least I had group medical coverage, for the first time in my life.)

Krisbaum was the one who informed me I was out of danger. Having a stomach full of sandwich had slowed my body's absorption of the poison.

My mouth and throat felt raw, but part of that may have been the stomach pump. My sinuses still hurt and I had a dull headache. I was feeling less optimistic than Krisbaum.

"Want me to contact your family?"

"No!" That was one trial I could spare myself.

"I know you don't want them worrying." Krisbaum shifted his bulk on the small bedside chair. "But they're bound to find out—"

"Not before I'm out of here. Not if you don't tell them." I groped on the night table for my dish of slivered ice. The nurses wouldn't give me water.

"It's not a matter of anybody *telling* them. You ate a sandwich prepared by Amanda McGuire—"

"Oh no! You're *not* going to arrest Mandy?"

"Well," Krisbaum said reasonably, "we did find hemlock in your stomach. And the only other thing you ingested today was a couple of Bloody Marys, right? Which you said three other people in your office shared. We're not ruling out the drinks yet—Kelly just ran the thermos over to the lab—but we do know nobody else got sick from them, not yet anyway. So if the thermos checks out . . ."

I looked out the hospital window. A hut-sized generator cast an outcropping of roof into shadow, blocking my afternoon light. "But Mandy wouldn't want to hurt me! She likes me!"

Krisbaum looked skeptical. Hard for him to believe anyone liked me, I guess. "We're not making any arrests right away. We'll wait on the lab reports and see what the fingerprint people turn up in your attorney lunchroom."

I felt slightly cheered. "Maybe someone *tampered* with the sandwich! Or the thermos, for that matter! Before I had the second drink."

"Never fear," he said dryly. "The thought did occur to us. You know what Justin Poat was in prison for, don't you?"

"Poat? Oh, I see. He could have stuck hemlock into the sandwich while Mandy was making it." I rubbed my aching sinuses. "Aggravated assault? Is that what they got him for?"

"You know who he assaulted?"

"Some bank officer? He went into a diatribe the other night about the bank's loan policies—how it wouldn't lend money to a chocolate-chip cookie store."

"He attacked a lady named Hannah Crosby."

"Hannah—! She's in-house counsel for California Bank and Trust!"

"That's right! She is now. She used to be one of their loan officers. Seven years ago, Poat parted her hair with a steel pipe. The pipe was packed with powder, supposed to be a bomb, but Poat screwed up the recipe. In his confession, he stated that when it didn't go off, he attacked the bank officer who personified the cruel disregard—I forget exactly how he put it."

"Hannah Crosby!" I sat forward too quickly, exposing an embarrassing strip of bare back under my hospital gown. "She was at the Mariposa retreat when Bob LeVoq—you know."

He stood up. "I'm aware of that."

I fumbled with the gown until my back was decently covered. "But it doesn't make sense! Why would Poat kill people in the law firm representing his enemy—or however Poat viewed Hannah? Why not just kill *her*?"

Krisbaum's eyelid twitched and he scowled down at me. "That's for the cops to think about, isn't it?" When I didn't reply, he repeated, more menacingly, "*Isn't* it?"

I picked up my dish of ice slivers only to find they'd melted. Disregarding nurses' orders, I drank the cold remains. "You'd have arrested Poat right off the bat if he'd killed Hannah. He's so strange. I wonder . . . maybe he's trying to get back at her in his own bizarre—" Seeing the expression on Krisbaum's face, I amended, "*If* it was him. Which is up to you to determine."

That wrung a reluctant grin out of him. "We try to be of service." With a showy bow, he left me to my conjectures.

36

I WOKE UP at dusk, surprised to find an East Indian
man standing over me, mumbling heavily accented
words of comfort. It wasn't until he produced a needle
that I remembered where I was. I offered my arm and
didn't bother stifling my yawn.

In the middle of a yawn that would have shamed a
hippopotamus, I noticed Don Surgelato standing in a
dark corner. He waited for the nurse to tape a wad of
cotton to my inner elbow. Then he stepped forward. He
looked angry, conspicuously waiting for the nurse to
leave.

I sat up, swallowing. My mouth and throat felt better,
but I knew I must look like hell. I brushed some hair
off my face and groped for the hand control that folded
the bed into a chaise. In the waning daylight, I looked
at Surgelato—curly black hair, thick brows, broken
nose, dimpled chin, five o'clock shadow. As the bed
rose to meet my back, I thought of all the times I'd
wandered North Beach, ogling Italian men. Even when

they weren't handsome, they had something. Maybe especially when they weren't handsome.

I didn't know what to say to him. He'd taken himself off my case. I was moving to Los Angeles. It was over before it started.

He pulled up a chair and sat close to my bed. "You feeling all right?"

"Yes. I'm okay. Have you talked to Krisbaum? Does he know—did the lab—"

He looked a little affronted. "I know more about this than Danny does, believe me."

"Let me rephrase the question: Do *you* know—"

"I heard Danny's tape," he said simply. "And I ordered him to stop running that bullshit on you."

"Because someone tried to kill me?"

"Because it's bullshit!" His brows sank so low they obscured his eyes.

"How close was it?" Part of me was morbidly curious; part of me didn't want to know. "How much hemlock did I eat?"

"Enough. As to how close—who knows? It acts quickly with some people. Others don't feel much effect for several hours. You didn't have breakfast this morning?"

"No."

He nodded, suspicion apparently confirmed.

"Lieutenant, I don't know how bad it gets, but I was feeling awful. And it was less than half an hour from the time I ate that sandwich to the time Krisbaum walked into my office."

He sighed, rubbing his eyes. "It's been known to be fatal in that amount of time."

"But why—?" I sat forward, drawing my knees up. "Say it is Poat. Why? Why should he want to poison me? Or William Mott, for that matter?"

"It could be a vendetta—"

"Against a law firm?"

"Against one of its clients."

"California Bank and Trust. I know Justin's weird about CBT, but killing off its outside counsel? What good would that do?"

Surgelato shrugged.

"You think Poat's crazy, don't you? That he didn't need a sane reason."

"That's my impression. But I'm not an expert."

I became aware of a chill on my back where the hospital gown hung open. Shivering, I reached over my shoulder to tug it closed.

A distracted frown on his face, Don Surgelato rose to help me.

His hand was warm on my skin as he pulled the halves together and fumbled to retie the laces. I looked up at him. He bent closer.

And a squeal of outrage filled the room.

Mother.

"Willa June! Do you know what this man has *done*?"

Surgelato took a giant step away from me.

"Retied my gown! What are you doing here, Mother?"

She dropped her plastic shopping bag and flew to me, clutching me in a weepy embrace. She smelled of incense and musty sweater.

I mumbled into her shoulder, "I asked Inspector Krisbaum not to tell you—"

She released me, staring at me with round, wet eyes. I've never seen her look more appalled. "You asked that, that—"

"Policeman!"

"—*fascist* to conceal this from me?" She made an operatic gesture, almost smacking my jaw in the process. "What's *happened* to you, Willa? How can you cast your lot with these people? Don't you know—"

Her eyes swam with tears; the loose flesh beneath her

chin trembled. "Do you know what this man did to us today?"

"Did to *you*? Did you have some kind of demonstration—'

Surgelato edged back into a shadowed corner. *Suspend Surgelato*. My mother was clever with slogans; I wondered if she'd coined that one.

"He smashed the commune!" She pulled herself erect, chin held high and eyes glittering. I almost expected her to burst into *The Marseillaise*.

"I'm sorry it came to that, Ms. Jansson. But given *this*"—Surgelato's voice made it plain I was the *this*— "I thought the precaution was necessary."

"Precaution!" Mother screamed. "That commune was the only real house those two sad, frightened people ever had. And for no reason at all—as a *precaution*—you've gone and—" she gulped back tears, her hands fluttering in the air—"tossed them out in the street."

"We didn't toss them into the street. We found alternative lodging—"

"Oooh!" she howled with furious contempt. "Is that what you call it? A firetrap full of prostitutes and drug addicts?" In other circumstances, Mother would have defended the innate goodness of prostitutes and drug addicts.

"Ms. Jansson!" Exasperation. "They're in one of the hotels you're trying to keep Malhousie Law School from tearing down!"

But Mother was not to be bested. "I'm not saying prostitutes don't have a right to a roof over their heads. I'm saying it's not the place for Mandy and Justin! They need a *home*. They need each other!"

"Right now—" There was a rumble of anger in Surgelato's voice. "I don't care *what* they need! There's too damn much hemlock near the bay! I don't want them in that neighborhood anymore! And if they're conspiring, I don't want them sharing quarters. I want them where we can keep an eye on them.'' He jerked one hand up, palm inward. Whatsa matter you? ''We're trying to keep your daughter alive!''

''You *see* what he's doing, Willa, don't you?'' Mother bent closer. I could smell black bean sauce on her breath. ''He's using an unobjectionable end as justification for unconscionable means!''

I was glad she found the end—keeping me alive—''unobjectionable.'' ''Mother, he hasn't arrested anyone. He's just trying to take precautions—''

''Precautions!'' Her voice was shrill enough to shatter glass. ''I hoped when you went to live with them—Oh, baby, didn't you get to know them at all?''

Baby—it hurt to hear her call me that. ''Yes, I did! I did get to know them! And they're not the''—I groped for the right word—''the *innocents* you think they are, Mother! They're—I don't know if they're crazy exactly, but—they're certainly on the edge!''

She straightened up, letting her arms drop to her side. She was through gesticulating; always a sign of deep disappointment. ''Of course they're on the edge, Willa! Wouldn't you be, if you'd just spent years in jail? But since when is that a crime? This man''—she glared at Surgelato—''has taken their stable environment away from them. Just because he can't see beyond their past mistakes! Which is exactly what I'd expect from *him*. The *him* dripped with contempt. ''I'd expect *him* to be blind to a person's true self! But *you*! Willa!'' Tears streamed down her face. ''You used to have a *heart*!''

Watching her cry for the heart I no longer had, I felt distanced from her. Once before she'd lavished sympathy on someone who'd tried—and narrowly failed—to kill me. Would her heart still bleed for Poat if it turned out he'd fed me hemlock? An epithet formed on my lips; not something you say to your own mother. I clamped my mouth shut.

Mother and I stared hostilely at one another. It was a second or two before I noticed the hospital room door swinging open.

A bright light flashed. As Surgelato moved toward the door, I strained my dazzled eyes to see beyond Mother. There were three or four of them in the hospital corridor, setting up lights and hoisting minicams, arguing with a uniformed officer and a nurse.

The press had found me.

Before Surgelato reached the door, my mother raced across the room and slipped through it. In the corridor, she clapped her hands and announced, "I have a statement I wish to make!"

Surgelato, obviously taken aback, watched from the doorway as the cameras ravened Mother. Too late to muscle her out of there. Too late to send the reporters away. Anything Surgelato did now would look like bullying.

I pulled the covers up around my neck. If I could see them, they could see me. The room was too dark for them to take pictures, and Don would keep them from entering. Still, as individuals, they could see me. It made me feel vulnerable, almost violated.

Mother, the veteran of many a Media Alliance, stood at the intersection of two bright lights, her spine straight and her neck long. The rise and fall of her shoulders told me she was breathing deeply, calming herself, striving for *samma sati*.

"My name is June Jansson," she proclaimed. "Tonight a great injustice"—all semblance of calm left her voice—"a *very great* injustice has been done! Homicide Lieutenant Surgelato has played judge and jury and taken it upon himself to ruin two young lives!"

Surgelato stepped forward, as if involuntarily. Then, realizing he was within camera range, he shrank back into the hospital room, closing the door behind him.

He turned around, leaning against the door. It was

almost dark in the room now, on the night side of dusk.
He was too far away for me to see his face.

My mother was in the corridor slandering him. I
didn't know what to say.

He didn't say anything, either.

He waited a few minutes, then he slipped through the
door. Mother was no longer talking, but the lights were
still on. The door wasn't open long enough for me to
see what was going on.

Alone, I finally spoke the epithet Mother had brought
to my lips.

37

Mother had done one thing right. She'd left behind the plastic shopping bag containing my sweat
clothes and People's Republic shoes. I put them on and
outwaited the newspeople. I told the nurse and the uniformed cop at the end of the corridor that they couldn't
keep me against my will, and I signed a bunch of forms
saying that whatever happened to me as a result of leaving without a doctor's okay, it was my own damn fault.

I called a cab, had it stop at a liquor store to pick up some empty cardboard boxes, and then had it cruise my apartment. No sign of reporters. They thought I was in the hospital.

Relieved, I carried the boxes upstairs, wondering if there was anything edible in my cupboards. It had been a long time since I'd eaten, and my last meal hadn't stayed with me.

I made my landlord unlock my door. He frowned at my cardboard boxes, obviously on the verge of asking about them. I slipped inside before he had a chance.

I found some canned hominy Daddy had brought over during a southern grits phase. I ate it cold out of the can, and decided General Sherman had the right idea.

Then I got stoned and did some packing; just clothes and books. I didn't care if I never saw my shabby furniture or mismatched dishes again. I was thirty-five, and I had nothing to show for it but a cheap wardrobe, some dusty books and a load of student debt.

I was done by eleven o'clock. It had taken me less than three hours to pack my worldly estate.

I sat on a box of books, looking around the living room. Spiders scrambled over disturbed bookcases. The floor was strewn with law school outlines and left-wing junk mail. The air smelled of musty paperbacks. It takes a hell of a mess to depress me, but this one did.

I put my phone back on the hook, and dialed Mother's Fresh Start Commune. No answer. Surgelato's men had rousted Justin and Mandy into separate rooms at a residence hotel; the commune was unoccupied. And tidy. I still had clothes there. There were clean sheets on "my" bed.

I called a cab, and had it take me there.

I let myself in and clicked on the hall light. The house was cold; someone, maybe Surgelato, had turned off the thermostat when he'd evicted the tenants. As I walked past the living room, I glanced in. Light spilled through the open door. In black and gray, with its cheap deco tables and stylized china panthers, its *TV Guide*s and easy chairs, it was like an old episode of *The Twilight Zone*.

I shook off a case of the creeps and headed for the kitchen. I swung the door open and looked into the small, tiled room. In the hallway light, it looked modern and cozy, very Julian Warneke. I could almost imagine his singing-bird tea kettle on the stove and his pasta-making machine on the butcher block table. I should have known what I'd find when I turned on the light.

Steaks of gray powder on the white tile, bits of litter on the linoleum, the refrigerator door ajar. I crossed to it, letting it swing open. Empty. I tried the oak cupboards. Cheap dishes and Safeway glasses. Not a crumb of food.

The cops had taken it all away.

I checked the back door and turned out the downstairs lights. I climbed the stairs. My mouth tasted gummy from the marijuana, my eyes felt scratchy and dry. I wanted to sleep.

I stopped on the upstairs landing. There was a light on in one of the rooms. I could see it filtering through the thin crack between the door and the frame. The long ray swirled with smoke. Pot smoke; I could smell it. It was "my" room; probably my pot, too. I'd tucked a couple of joints between the mattress and the box spring.

I considered turning around and leaving. It couldn't be a police guard; Mother would never allow one in the house. Besides, there wasn't anything left to guard. The food had been packed off to a police lab. Mandy and Justin had been deposited in a cheap hotel, their possessions doubtless rifled and their rooms searched. Besides, a cop wouldn't smoke my pot.

I turned quietly around, starting back down the stairs.

If the intruder had come to search my room—to read the files in my briefcase, perhaps?—why would he (she?) smoke my pot? I paused, hand on the railing.

Maybe Mother had installed a Salvadoran refugee in the house.

I looked over my shoulder. Whoever it was, he couldn't mean to harm me. He wouldn't be smoking pot if he did. Pot isn't conducive to belligerence.

On the other hand, I didn't want to cope with one of Mother's illegals. I wasn't sure I could get my brain to click into Spanish anymore.

Spanish turned out to be unnecessary. I heard footsteps across the braided carpet of my room. I wheeled around to face whoever came out the door.

It swung open, lighting the upstairs landing and, less brilliantly, the stairs. A man stepped out of my room, a stack of file folders in his hand. For some reason, it was the file folders I noticed first; that bit of daily life— *my* life—in someone else's hand.

I looked up. He stood there clutching my files, frozen in a smoky shaft of light.

Wild-haired and dressed in an out-of-style, too-big suit, Justin Poat looked just as surprised as I did.

"I thought—"

"Thought I was sup-supposed to be gone!" Justin raised the files, flapping them like a broken wing. "To a bug-eaten hotel!"

"Are you—? I won't tell anyone, but are you supposed to be here? Did the police say you could come back?"

"The *police*? You know what they call the 'police' at Soledad? Yes!" As he approached the stairs his voice got louder. "I'm violating my parole. They could send me back to jail, just for coming to this house. Just for talking to you! Just for doing, just for—" His voice throbbed with grievance. He stood a dozen steps above me, waving the files.

"I won't tell anyone!" I repeated, backing down another step.

"You're good at not telling! You didn't tell me you were whoring for the bank!" He tossed the files down at me. The manila corners caught me hard against the cheek before flying over the banister.

I turned, stumbling quickly down the remaining stairs. Poat was shouting now, something about *knowing* it—me with my suits and my fucking high heels telling him to cooperate with the cops and sitting in my room with the door closed like I'd get lice or something talking to the jailbirds.

I managed to reach the hall before I heard him cannon down the stairs.

The front door was too far away. I knew I wouldn't make it. I dashed into the living room and slammed the door shut, wedging my body against it at the same instant Poat barreled into it. He knocked me back half a foot, but I got the door closed again. I braced myself for another blow. Instead I heard Poat shuffle his feet, draw a rasping breath.

He muttered something. At first I couldn't make it out. I was gulping air, my heart hammering.

He muttered louder, "The gunpowder was damp, they said it was damp. Supposed to seal it. I shouldn't be here now. Should have been my swan song. My statement. I waited and waited. Then she comes and sneers at me: Why aren't I working? What am I waiting for? Long-haired bitch. I was going to die for her, and she sneers at me. And doesn't even bleed! She doesn't even bleed! I spend seven years, one month and six fucking days scared to shit. Scared to talk, scared to move, scared to eat my goddam food!"

I could hear him pacing the hall. How long had he known I worked for Hannah Crosby, the long-haired bitch who'd had the temerity not to bleed when he hit her with a pipe bomb?

Out there, pacing, pacing. Was he paranoid enough
to blame me by extension? To spike my sandwich with
hemlock?

The pacing stopped. He hit the door again. I wasn't
prepared for it. The impact sent me staggering backward, into a sharp corner of the coffee table. Groping
for balance, my fingers encountered one of the ceramic
panthers. I hurled it at Poat as I fell over the table.

I smashed my shoulder on the couch and wrenched
my knee. In the unlighted room, in a tangle of limbs
between the table and sofa, I couldn't tell where Poat
was in relation to me. I pushed the table away and
scrabbled to my knees. The man was insane, no doubt
about it; and if he decided to hit me, he'd make damn
sure I bled.

I blinked, struggling to focus my night vision. He
seemed to be beside the door, stooping, his hands on
his head. It might be a psychotic break, voices in his
head; or maybe I'd hit him with the panther. I didn't
care which.

I got up, ran into the dining room and out that door,
into the hall. I was afraid to backtrack past the living
room, past Poat. I darted into the kitchen.

I could hear the scrape of Poat's feet and an explosion
of profanity as I fumbled with the back door lock.

But I was outside and down the back stairs before
Poat could follow.

Or maybe he did follow. I was running so fast I didn't
hear anything but my own panting on that understatedly
elegant street.

I didn't turn around until I reached a chichi oyster
bar. One hand on the brass door handle, I scanned the
lamplighted street. Six-foot trees fluttered, a cat slid
under a car. I was alone.

I stepped into the bar and collapsed into a Victorian
couch. There was someone at the other end, a heavily
madeup woman with dramatic chin-length hair. All

around me on couches and bar stools, well-groomed women conversed with men in black tie or artistic dishabille. Cigarette smoke mingled with the medicine smell of liqueur and the bilge smell of oysters.

"What can I get you?" a cheerful, bearded man inquired.

"A phone book."

Looking less cheerful, he pointed to an alcove with a telephone.

Surgelato was in the White Pages, thank goodness; a classy North Beach address. A short cab ride, in fact. I didn't care what he thought of the idea. I needed to see him someplace other than a hospital or a police station.

38

I T WAS A house. An entire house in a neighborhood where houses were divided into pricy cubicles. A three-story brick rowhouse on a street of Italian bakeries and all-night bookstores. The air smelled of Graffeo coffee and salted olives, of bay wind and night traffic. The streets were full of people—fur coats rushing to Tosca's to mingle with opera singers; poets shambling to City Lights Books to philosophize; conventioneers straying from joints with blinking nipples on the marquees. Not the daytime crowd of matrons in black Italian knits, of Chinese men in fedoras, of curly-haired boys in deli aprons.

From Surgelato's alabaster stairs I could see Washington Square, with its tidy walks and old-fashioned statues, its lasso of headlights inching toward the bay. Surgelato could probably see the bridge from his top-floor window.

I pressed the doorbell. Maybe I'd live in a place with only one doorbell, someday.

What was it my landlord told me? Surgelato's family owned a bank?

I heard footsteps tripping down stairs. They stopped at the door. I was conscious of being scrutinized through a magnifying peephole. You'd think a homicide lieutenant would be more fearless.

I guess I didn't look very menacing. Surgelato opened the door.

"What the *hell*—" he said inhospitably. "Who authorized your release?"

"From the hospital?" I felt myself take an unconscious step backward. He hadn't sent someone to arrest me, had he?

He grabbed my elbow and pulled me inside. "From the lunatic asylum! What are you doing here?"

We were in a walnut-paneled atrium hung with watercolors of the bay. There was a closed door to my right and a staircase behind him. Mellow light from brass sconces. In the fake candlelight, he looked quite handsome.

For one thing, he wasn't wearing a suit. He was built wrong for a suit, too broad of chest, too short of leg. He looked better now, in jeans and a sweater with a V of hairy chest showing (and no gold chains, thank god). His hair was in damp, spiky curls, and he needed a shave. He didn't look like a homicide lieutenant. He looked like the cute waiter at Caffe Roma.

"Something happened. I wanted to tell you about it."

Surgelato glanced up the stairs, scowling. He'd dropped in on me plenty of times in the course of his investigations; I thought he might have been a bit more gracious.

Then a woman appeared at the top of the stairs. An imposing brunette with Loretta Lynn hair and a tightly belted red sweater. "Oh, great!" She seemed to fling the words downstairs. "Another miniature blonde!" She wheeled around and vanished beyond the horizon of stair.

"Christina," he explained bitterly. He seemed to think the name meant something to me.

I'd been blaming my mother—and the circumstances of Julian's murder—for Surgelato's coolness. I hadn't factored in prior claims by an angry brunette.

"Maybe I should go talk to Inspector Krisbaum."

"No. Come on." He took my arm and guided me up the thickly carpeted steps. You don't see that kind of carpeting in rentals.

The staircase led to a huge white-walled living room with several sofas and chairs, no two of the same (expensive) fabric or color. They were arranged in random groupings around mismatched cocktail tables. There were dozens of watercolors on the walls, mostly of blue sky and calm water. The brunette was standing under one of the larger ones, crankily hugging herself.

"Ms. Jansson is here on business, Tina." Surgelato's tone was dangerously patronizing.

" 'Thank you, ma'am,' " she replied ironically. She glanced at me, smiling slightly when I recognized part three of the sailors' jingle.

Surgelato ran an angry hand over his hair. Again the patronizing tone: "I'll walk you to your car."

"Carry my books, too?" Her soft voice implied a sentimental journey.

Judging from his scowl, the lieutenant wasn't feeling sentimental.

She bent over the cocktail table and picking up a Gucci bag and patting a stack of books. Hardcovers; probably textbooks.

Surgelato took the cue, crossing to the cocktail table and picking up the books. As he straightened, she clutched his arm. "You're punishing me for something I didn't even do!"

Surgelato turned his back on me. "I told you—it wasn't a question of *doing* anything!" He sounded embarrassed.

The woman's cheeks flushed, and she was suddenly gorgeous. "It's what I *didn't* do. I didn't keep my mouth shut and pass around tiny meatball hors d'oeuvres. I didn't disappear into the kitchen during parties. I tried to get to know your friends!"

"Oh, Christ!" Surgelato walked briskly toward the stairs, eyes on the carpet as he passed me.

Christina followed more slowly, stopping to inspect me. "There hasn't been a Surgelato woman in ten generations who's had fun at a party. It's undignified." Fishing keys out of her bag, she stepped closer. We were almost nose to nose. Her eyes sparkled; she seemed to be enjoying herself. "And Donnie," she concluded, "embarrasses very easily!"

I heard Surgelato mutter an oath from somewhere on the stair. Christina walked past me, joining him there.

Before the front door slammed, I heard him say, "For god's sake, Tina!"

I curled up in a duckcloth chair and stared at one of the watercolors: a boat becalmed. Working in Homicide must make a person long for tranquility.

Donnie embarrasses easily. A pot-smoking murder suspect with loudmouthed radical parents might be something of an embarrassment at the Policeman's Ball.

Just as well I was going to L.A.

I bit my lips and slapped my cheeks. Surgelato was not going to find me crying.

Ten minutes later, when he ran up the stairs, I was still telling myself to buck up.

He crouched in front of me. "You sure you're okay? You checked with a doctor about side effects?"

"My throat hurts. That's about it." I sat up, facing him. No use getting too comfortable. "I went to Mother's commune to pick up some things I still had there—"

"Jesus! What are you running all over town for? Especially at night? You're a native—does this seem like a safe city to you? *Especially* to you? Especially right now?"

"I packed my sheets. I needed a bed—"

"Packed your—? What did you do that for?"

"I'm moving to L.A."

He stood up, shaking his head. "You're not leaving town till this is cleared up!"

"I can't wait too long. They might change their minds about having me."

" 'They' being?"

"Wailes, Roth in L.A. If I don't transfer to the L.A. office it'll look like a vote of no confidence on their part. Like they don't trust me. I won't be able to get a job representing the dog catcher!"

He rubbed his brows. "L.A."

"I don't have any choice!"

"If we clear you—"

"It won't make any difference. I have to prove my next boss won't drop dead. If I don't continue at Wailes I might as well put a skull and crossbones on my résumé!"

He flopped into the nearest chair. "All right. I can see that." I thought he looked relieved.

"Was that woman your ex-wife?"

He nodded.

"You told me about her once. You said she acted too charming at parties."

"Not charming. Amusing. At my expense." He changed the subject. "You were saying . . . something happened at your Mother's commune?"

"Justin Poat was there."

"*What?*" He leaped out of his chair and crossed to a black telephone. "Poat's supposed to be downtown at the American Hotel." He dialed quickly. "And somebody's supposed to be watching the place to make sure he stays there!" He spoke into the receiver. "Surgelato. Willa Jansson says she saw Poat at One Twenty-eight Filene—that's right, the 'fresh start' place. So what the hell happened to Kelly?" Silence. "Check it out. Both places. I'll be there in a while."

He hung up, turning back to me. "What was Poat doing?"

"He was going through my files. My case files. When he saw me, he—He kind of went nuts. He started chasing me around." I considered telling him about the pot. It usually calms people down. Just my luck it made Poat paranoid.

"What exactly did Poat do?"

"He threw my files at me—California Bank and Trust files—then he chased me downstairs. I ran into the living room and closed the door, but he knocked it open." I rubbed my leg where I'd slammed it into the coffee table. "I threw a statuette at him and ran out the back door."

"What were his intentions? What do you think he was going to do to you?"

"He was raving about the bank, about me working

for it. I thought—'' God, my mother would kill me for saying so. "I thought he was going to hit me."

"Give me a minute to change. I want you to come down to the Hall with me."

I stood up, blocking his path as he walked past my chair. "Don?"

He looked startled that I'd used his given name.

"I'm sorry my mother said all those things about you."

He shrugged. He would have continued past, but I put my hand on his arm. "I wish we could talk."

He looked away, at a painting of sunny sea. "You're a lawyer. You think that's such a good idea?"

The Suspend Surgelato Committee believed he'd had an ulterior motive for shooting Warneke's killer. Even Krisbaum believed Surgelato's relationship with me had been a factor.

I took my hand off his arm and let him go change his clothes.

39

KRISBAUM WAS TRYING to act nonchalant. "So how come you went to the lieutenant's place?"

Everything had worn off: the pot, the adrenaline, the false hopes for romance.

"You forget our address?"

And now I had to put up with Krisbaum's sense of humor.

"I just went. I didn't analyze the impulse."

"You've been there before, I take it?"

After staring at him for an hour (a whole hour we'd talked about Justin Poat, his every utterance and gesture), I itched to straighten Krisbaum's tie. "No. I've never been there before."

He feigned surprise. "Never been there? But Don was telling me . . ." He waited, bait dangling. I must look stupid. "So how did you find the place?"

"White Pages of the telephone book. Clever, huh?"

We were in a tiny interrogation room, as usual. Krisbaum made a production of studying some spots in the white cork soundproofing. He rubbed his chin. "I'm going to get a little personal now." A smiling glance. "You don't mind."

If that was supposed to be subliminal persuasion, he wasn't very good at it. "I do mind."

He shifted his chair so that it was around the corner from mine, rather than across the big table. "Let's look at it another way. The way the commissioner is inclined to look at it." He let that one hang in the air for a minute. "Not that he wants to second-guess us publicly—not yet."

I waited, allowing Krisbaum his pregnant pause.

"But he's done it before, Miss Jansson."

"I'm aware of that." The commissioner had ordered my arrest for the murder of Julian Warneke. Surgelato had carried out the order.

"Well, look at it this way. We didn't find any traces of hemlock anywhere in your office."

"You didn't?"

"No. We didn't."

I rubbed my eyes. "Just tell me what's on your mind. I'm not feeling very sharp-witted."

"You know, we've got marijuana with your name on it in the evidence locker."

"My name?"

"From your mother's commune. I told them to tag the pot as yours. That's right, isn't it? It's your pot?"

"I'm not saying it is or it isn't. Are you busting me?"

"No. I'm just telling you, it could be used to show mental instability."

"If you arrest me for murder."

"Yes."

"I didn't kill anyone. I'm just"—it sounded stupid, but I believed it—"I'm cursed. Besides, how do you account for the fact that I was poisoned—" I gaped at him, finally getting his point. "You think I ate it myself. On purpose. To throw you off the track!"

"I didn't say *I* thought so."

"Well, if the commissioner thinks so, he's—"

"My boss!" Krisbaum flushed with irritation. "Look at the facts: you ingest all the hemlock on the scene, and you do it with people around so that at the first peep of a complaint you get rushed downstairs to get your stomach pumped. Now *someone*"—his tone said, *maybe even me*—"might think the whole thing was staged."

"*Someone* might be an idiot. Did you check the waxed paper from Mandy's sandwich? The Bloody Mary cups?"

Krisbaum nodded.

"Melinda's thermos? LeVoq's wife was alone in the reception room with the thermos—"

"Tomato juice, V-8, lime, tabasco, and vodka. Period." He grinned wryly. "And yes, we had a look around Mrs. LeVoq's house and Miss Karastatos' apartment."

I had a disquieting thought. "Are you going to search my apartment?"

"They're doing that now."

As if on cue, someone tapped at the door. Krisbaum excused himself and left me sitting there lamenting the packing his minions were now undoing.

Krisbaum was back in less than a minute. He had a small zip-lock plastic bag in his hand, the kind pot comes in these days. It looked empty. But when he tossed it in front of me, I could see a whitish smear and some grainy lumps. It looked like a bit of mashed pear—

"Oh, don't tell me! Hemlock! They found hemlock root in my apartment!"

Krisbaum held up his other hand, showing me a small tape recorder. He spoke into it. "For the record, this is San Francisco Police Inspector Daniel J. Krisbaum. I am interviewing Willa June Jansson . . ."

I listened to the rest of the stats: my address, my age, the date, the time. And of course, my rights. They have to read you your rights when an interrogation becomes "custodial"—when you can't leave just because you want to. Krisbaum wasn't arresting me; he'd have said so, if he was. But the character of the interview had changed. He wasn't just getting information; he was making a record to use against me.

"I have no idea how that got into my apartment. I left there at around eleven o'clock tonight—last night, I should say—and I haven't been back. Someone must have planted it there."

Krisbaum was frowning. "You have somebody in mind?"

I hated like hell to say it. "Bud Hopper."

Krisbaum sighed.

"Well, not Hopper, but whoever identified himself as Hopper to Thomas Spender and William Mott, and got me this job. Except—" I traced a crack in the wood table. It went a certain distance, then stopped abruptly. "Mott said he'd never talked to Hopper. Somebody else must have. Or claimed to. And told Mott about it!" I covered my eyes. Maybe the fluorescence was affecting my deductive ability. "Have you found the real Bud Hopper yet?"

He sat back in his chair, chewing the inside of his cheek. "As a matter of fact, we have."

I was almost afraid to ask. "He's never heard of me, has he?"

Reluctantly, Krisbaum shook his head.

"I knew it!" I felt the sting of relieved tears. "I told you! Someone used his name and his credentials to get me an interview with Wailes, Roth. Someone told William Mott that Hopper wanted me to go to that awful retreat. And Hopper's never even heard of me! I'm being framed!"

Krisbaum grimaced. "I'll tell you something, Miss

Jansson. Thomas Spender doesn't remember why the hell the firm hired you. Says he gets recommendations all the time from all kinds of people."

"But the L.A. partners will tell you: Mott and I talked about it at the retreat. The first night, at dinner."

"Where *you* brought it up, I don't doubt."

"Ask Melinda! Ask the L.A. partners! I wouldn't have been invited to the retreat if this false Hopper hadn't called and—"

"I'm not saying I doubt you. I'm just wondering if it's as important as you think it is."

"Yes!" I said positively. "Someone's copying the Warneke murder and framing me for it!"

"And what happened yesterday—you eating hemlock? That doesn't sound like much of a frame."

"Let me think about this."

"Think about this, too, Miss Jansson: you're smart enough to make a phone call identifying yourself as someone you're not."

"Why would *I* want to set myself up?"

He shook his head impatiently. "Not set yourself up. Just get yourself a good job."

"And then I suppose I just couldn't resist killing my new boss?"

Krisbaum tapped the plastic baggie. "This hemlock was found smeared on the pull-out cutting board—"

"The what?"

"Cutting board? Wooden thing next to the sink you pull out from under the counter? Little built-in job you find in older places? To cut your bread on?"

"There's a cutting board next to my sink?"

"Come on!" He looked irritated, his skin reddening in damp patches. "Are you telling me you don't know whether there's a cutting board in your kitchen?"

"Of course I don't know. I never cut anything. Except microwave bags."

He all but rolled his eyes. "Well, actually, you may

or may not have a cutting board in the kitchen of your apartment. This''—he tapped the baggie again—''was scraped off the cutting board at One Twenty-eight Filene—''

''Mother's commune!''

''That's right. Lab just analyzed it. It looks like your sandwich was the culprit, after all.''

''But Mandy wouldn't have—''

''Amanda McGuire wasn't the only person with access to that kitchen, Miss Jansson.''

40

WHILE KRISBAUM AND I wrangled about Bud Hopper, two uniformed cops charged into the American Hotel, dragged Justin Poat out of bed and pushed him through the corridor, beating him with nightsticks as he struggled. ''Resisting arrest'' was enough to get his parole revoked. He was also charged with murder and attempted murder.

Unfortunately, I heard about it from my mother.

I was repacking the things I'd packed the night before, tossing in towels without folding them, shoes without wrapping them. I felt like hell after half a night of Krisbaum, and I'd gotten a call at eight in the morning from Melinda, anxious to find out how I was feeling. She told me L.A. had accepted her ultimatum. They wanted us to fly down as soon as possible. They'd formulated a strategy for keeping some of San Francisco's bigger cases.

Whoopee.

Mother arrived while I was repacking books.

I was sitting in a cloud of dust when she unlocked my door with her key. She never bothered knocking; she only respected privacy in principle.

She stood over me in her ancient bell-bottoms and flowered shirt, her flyaway hair in clownish disarray, her brow puckered in furious disapproval. She'd have scared the crap out of John Brown himself.

"Willa June! You've destroyed two lives! Two of God's children—" Her breath caught. Too angry to speak; that was a new one.

"You're not talking about Mott and LeVoq, are you?" It was the faintest hope. If she considered me a murderess, I might win her pity.

"Justin Poat is no more capable of harming anyone than—"

"He tried to blow up a bank and everybody in it, Mother!"

"Seven years ago! And don't you try to tell me seven years of guilt and agony don't expiate—"

"I'm not trying to tell you anything!" I stood up, wiping my hands on my sweatpants. "*I* didn't arrest Poat, you know!"

"You did something worse! Morally worse! You gave information against him!"

"The police found hemlock on his cutting board. Also"—I straightened my spine, preparing for a storm—

"he attacked me last night." In her frenzy of compassion for Poat, would she even care?

Mother shook her head emphatically. "Whatever you *think* he was trying to do, he *wasn't*!"

"How do *you* know? *You*'ve never lived with him. The man's nuts!"

She took a step closer. "Willa, listen to me—you haven't spent as much time in prison as I have! Justin's sickness is something that's endemic in there! Like head lice!"

"Oh, *please*! He attacked someone with a pipe bomb! And probably spent all of one hour a year with a psychiatrist since then! And you're telling me he's just, just—what? Adjusting?"

"Adjusting. That's exactly right, Willa! He spent seven years in hell!" Her lower lip began to tremble, her chest to heave. "And now they've sent him back! Oh, dear merciful Lord!" She turned away from me, crossing herself over and over again. Her shoulders hunched; she was weeping.

I leaned wearily against the bookcase, watching her. Somewhere along the line, I'd stopped believing in the innate goodness of the Justin Poats of the world. And I'd started trusting the police. No use trying to comfort Mother. The news was worse than she feared.

"Mandy," she hiccuped, "Mandy's had a nervous breakdown." She turned around, wiping her wet lashes. "She went into the hotel lobby and saw them beating Justin with their nightsticks! She'll never—I don't think she'll ever—"

If I could have backed farther away from her I would have. Justin had attacked me; I wasn't roused to pity him. But Mandy was another matter. Mandy had baked me cookies. She'd made my bed every morning. Hung up those pathetic calendar towels. Jesus, poor woman.

Mother seemed to sense her advantage. She moved in for the kill. "But you don't care. You go to the gestapo with the vaguest accusations, and what do they do? They beat an innocent man insensate. They destroy the fragile sanity of a woman who was finally starting—'' She swallowed, looking around the box-filled room. ''You can't run away from what you've done to them, Willa!''

''I'm not running away. I'm moving to Los Angeles.''

Mother's eyes narrowed.

''Wailes, Roth's San Francisco office folded. I've been transferred to L.A.''

She stared at me, her cheeks wet, her chest still heaving. But she didn't comment. She didn't have to. I knew what Wailes, Roth represented to her.

She left without saying good-bye.

41

IT WAS A bright, windy day. I walked down the panhandle toward Haight Street. There were roller skaters on the walkways. A wet lawn smell in the air.

It was twenty years ago today. The words of the Bea-

tles song were splashed across magazine covers in
Haight Street news stands. The summer of love.

Easy to be nostalgic about it.

Getting high was great. Unsafe sex was fun. Jimi
Hendrix and Janis Joplin and Arlo Guthrie were terrific.
The Avalon Ballroom's light shows were the best. But
love? As I remembered that summer, it was men versus
women, students versus administration, radicals versus
liberals, Trotskyites versus radicals, them versus us.
There was hardly anyone I didn't hate, that summer.

I meandered up Haight. The last few years had
brought in dozens of new businesses; storefronts were
freshly painted, copper-and-brass espresso machines
gleamed on café counters, shop windows showcased
Italian shoes, hardcover best-sellers, gourmet kitchen-
ware and lobster bibs. I stood a hundred yards from the
Haight-Ashbury Free Clinic and let the stylish crowd
flow around me. The place looked like Berkeley. Chic,
bustling, colorful.

It used to be the smell of patchouli from head shops,
a hip malt shop, used bookstores, kids in moccasins
one-upping their Ohio peers, *The Berkeley Barb* thrust
through gawkers' car windows. Being fifteen, full of
interesting drugs and political energy, had made the
experience fun.

But at thirty-five, feeling dispirited and tired, I could
see that the Haight suited me better now. People
weren't talking politics on every street corner, but they
weren't squabbling and bickering about incremental re-
form versus a general strike, either. They wanted some
creature comforts. I did, too.

On impulse, I turned the corner. A friend of mine
lived a few doors down from the Free Clinic. When I
first met Manuel Boyd he'd been a reporter for a free
tabloid called the *Express*. His stories about the "law
school murders," as they'd been called, had won him
a spot on San Francisco's morning paper. He'd helped

me unravel the mess surrounding Julian Warneke's murder, and I'd been a little surprised not to hear from him after Bob LeVoq's murder.

Manuel was old Haight. He scorned the "overpriced gelato" character of the neighborhood. Maybe it would bring some of the feeling back, talking to him.

I rang his bell, opening the downstairs door when I got a responding buzz.

But it turned out Manuel's neighbor had buzzed me in. For the last week, he'd buzzed in everyone who rang Manuel's bell. He told me what he'd been telling everyone else: Manuel Boyd had died of AIDS.

42

I RODE THE elevator to the twentieth floor of the California Street building. No cop waited in the hall to turn me away. I reached the massive door with the brass plate that read *Wailes, Roth, Fotheringham & Beck*, and I tried my key. The lock hadn't been changed.

Melinda Karastatos was in the reception room. She looked startled, even frightened when I stepped in.

"Oh, it's you!" She dropped an empty cardboard box and came closer, studying my face. "Do you feel okay? I didn't mean for you to come in today. I just meant as soon as you could, so we could get down there before—" She frowned pessimistically. "But I suppose we've lost them, no matter what we do."

"Our clients?"

"World Financial sent over a messenger this morning to pick up its files." She raised her hand, fingers curling as if to strike the messenger. She turned away.

I thought of my deposition of Dean Grenville, I'd been so damned careful to make a complete record. And now some other firm would use the information I'd elicited; maybe use it to win the case. Use it to please the client and enhance their own professional reputation.

I felt myself grow hot with indignation. World Financial was *our* client, damn it—*my* client.

Melinda continued gruffly. "Everything's pretty much accounted for, at this point. The files are copied and the boxes are marked. Clients who want to bail out now will have to phone L.A."

Unsure whether it was the right thing to say, I offered, "Congratulations on making partner."

She flashed me an over-the-shoulder grin. "It's like finding out your jewelry didn't melt in the fire that destroyed your house." She picked up the box she'd dropped when I walked in. "Come to my office for a few minutes."

I followed her in. Her bookcase was empty, stacks of books all over the floor. Atop one stack I noticed William Mott's signed photograph of Gerald Ford.

She sank into her leather chair and said, "I hate L.A. Not just the city, but the office. The office politics."

I sat opposite her. "Tell me about it."

She waved vaguely at her plaid thermos. "Just V-8 juice, but help yourself. I guess it's obvious Milward

Kael is the kingpin down there. He's all right." She
pushed the thermos toward me. "Sensible, nonpartisan.
Good at client development. Jonathan Seeder's a snake
in the grass, though!" She pulled back the thermos,
opened it and poured some juice into the cup. Then she
rummaged through her drawers until she found a coffee
mug and she filled that, too. She handed me the thermos cup and took a sip from the mug. "Seeder was
LeVoq's mentor—which just about says it all. He got
LeVoq made partner a year early so that there'd be a
partner up in this office. And since he'd put himself on
the line for Bob, he was determined to make everyone
think LeVoq was the Great White Litigator."

"I got that impression." I told her about my interview dinner in L.A.

She sat forward, nodding. "I got that 'rainmaker'
shit from Seeder, too. Four years I carried Bob on my
shoulders, and the whole time he's going down to
L.A. taking credit for my work—and telling the partners I'm insubordinate!" She stared with cold fury at
the contents of her coffee cup. "A 'rainmaker'! I told
Seeder—I told all of them—Bob couldn't make rain
with a garden hose!"

"What did they say?"

I settled in for a cozy gossip, sipping the tomato
cocktail (I didn't remember V-8 being so damned hot)
and wondering what I'd let myself in for, agreeing to
move to L.A.

We were well into the character assassination of var-
ious partners when a young man appeared at the open
door. Shabby jeans and long hair gave him a starving-
student air. "Is one of you Willa June Jansson?"

Willa June. Only my mother called me that. "Yes."

He looked relieved. "I've got a box for you. Want
me to carry it in here?"

"No. I'll show you where to put it."

I preceded him out of Melinda's office and waited

while he picked up a battered cardboard box. I led him down the hall to my office and told him to put the box on my desk. I only tipped him a dollar, trusting Mother had overpaid him, as she did everyone who did her a service.

When he left, I broke Mother's masking tape seal (no nonbiodegradable plastic tapes for her) and looked inside.

I sank into my chair. Stuff from "my" room at my parents' house. A change of clothes, slippers, hairbrush, batik bedspread, odds and ends. And a poster tube.

I pulled out the tube, feeling like I'd swallowed a coal. How could she take down my posters? They'd been on those walls for twenty years. *Twenty years ago today* . . .

My face felt hot, my eyes wet. She'd gotten back at me, all right.

I pulled out the posters. The one thing that had been right about those years was my mother. Mother and Daddy. Intelligent, committed, there when I wanted to talk, leaving me alone when I came home stoned, getting me birth control pills when it became clear I needed them.

I unfurled the posters. Topmost, no doubt by arrangement, was one of my newer posters, circa 1971. It was designed to look like a picture background bank check. Printed in the bottom left corner was the Bank of America logo and the address of its Isla Vista branch. There was a picture behind the date, dollars and signature lines: the Isla Vista branch aflame after a firebombing by radical students.

Mother bought me the poster as a coming-home present. I'd just spent two months in the San Bruno Jail for public obscenity and resisting arrest. Mother was sorry I'd had to miss the bank bombing.

I wiped my eyes. If she was trying to make me feel

awful, she was succeeding. My throat burned, my stomach was jumpy, my sinuses hurt. Crying was aggravating yesterday's ailment, but I couldn't seem to stop.

I'd left the San Bruno Jail determined never to end up behind bars again. I wasn't sorry I'd missed the bank bombing; I was weak-kneed with relief I hadn't been there.

But walking out of that tomb and into my parents' arms—Mother with the poster in one hand and a banana bread in the other, Daddy full of Thoreau and warm tears, the feel of four arms around me holding onto me—

I let my head sink onto the desktop and I cried. Cried till I felt like hell.

I felt weak when I sat up again. I started flipping through the other posters, hard-to-read psychedelic classics that were now collectors' items. Big Brother and the Holding Company at the Avalon. The Grateful Dead. The Doors.

I mopped my eyes with the tail of my batik bedspread and put the posters back in the box.

I felt rotten. I considered calling a cab and going home.

But I didn't have much packing to do—one advantage of having the job less than a month. Half an hour should do it. Then I could leave and stay gone.

I started packing, deliberately turning my back on Mother's box. I had enough problems without stewing about Mother.

I had Bud Hopper to worry about. Or rather, Hopper's impersonator.

I believed Justin Poat had tried to kill me. He was crazy enough—and shrewd enough—to copy a pattern of murder established by someone else. But I wasn't sure he'd killed Mott or LeVoq.

No, whatever Krisbaum might think, the Hopper im-

personation was the key. I'd been hired on a false recommendation to a New York partner. William Mott had
then been told (by whom?) that Hopper wanted me at
the retreat. LeVoq's murderer had obviously selected
hemlock as the poison of choice because of me, because my last boss had died that way. And photographing LeVoq on my bed, that had been a way of suggesting
a relationship between us—a motive for murder.

I mopped my face again. It was so damned hot in the
office; I was feeling a little light-headed.

No, the picture of LeVoq—it did more than suggest
a relationship. It made LeVoq look sleazy. That was the
first thing Krisbaum had commented.

Plenty of people at the retreat might have reveled in
making LeVoq look sleazy. His cuckolded wife. Maybe
his lover. Certainly his business associates.

I wondered who'd made the firm's reservations.
Whether it had been prearrangement or a lucky chance
that put me into that exposed first-floor room.

I coughed, testing my voice. The crying jag had left
it raw and whispery.

I picked up the phone and was surprised to hear a
woman say, ''Answering service.''

''Answering—? Can't I get an outside line?''

''We were told to hold all your calls unless someone
specifically asked to ring through to your office.''

''Oh.'' I appreciated Melinda's rationale for the arrangement. No reporters bothering us. No panicked clients. ''I'd like to call out.''

''Wait a second.'' I heard some clicking and a grunt.
Then a dial tone. ''Go ahead.''

My outside line survived a call to information. I got
the Mariposa's number and phoned the reservation desk.
I had to swallow twice before I could identify myself
as Wailes, Roth's office manager. I asked the reservation clerk to look up the information I needed: Who

made reservations for the retreat? Did that person request specific room assignments?

My mouth was watering, my tongue swelling. Delayed reaction? Was that possible? A relapse?

The clerk was less than cooperative, but I finally convinced her to do it. She put me on hold, and I listened to a syrupy instrumental version of "Yesterday."

The sinuses above my eyes were beginning to ache, as if they were swelling and pressing on my eyeballs. My nose was running. The phone cradled against my shoulder, I tossed the last of my books into a box. My next call would be for a taxi, to take me and my three boxes home.

The reservation clerk came back on. "Reservations were made by telephone. We have no record of who made them."

"Was the call from San Francisco or L.A.?"

"I have no way of knowing."

I hung up. Down the hall, I could hear water running. I looked at the phone, not wanting to hassle with having the answering service get me another outside line. There are plenty of cabs cruising the financial district. I'd label my boxes, go hail a cab, and find some starving student of my own to come back for my stuff.

I got up, paused for a few seconds with my hand on my belly, then walked carefully out of the office. Maybe it was the flu. On top of yesterday's hemlock and the fight with my mother—

I followed the sound of running water. Melinda must be in the attorneys' lounge. I wanted to say good-bye before I left. Explain about the boxes I was leaving behind.

I found her where I expected to find her: standing at the lounge sink, with her back to me. She was rinsing out her thermos, soaping and resoaping it, squirting liquid dish-soap into the sink where the tomato juice had splashed.

I was about to interrupt her when I noticed the thermos. It came briefly into view as she sloshed sudsy water in it, shaking it back and forth.

My mind's eye reconstructed a scene: Melinda pouring out Bloody Marys the day before. Pouring me a final drink half an hour before Krisbaum joined me. Pouring from the very thermos she was now washing.

Melinda hadn't shared that last drink with me. If hemlock had been added to the thermos after the communal toast—

But Krisbaum said the police lab had tested the thermos, and found no trace—Of course, that's what was bothering me. If the cops took Melinda's thermos away for testing, how could she have it now?

I backed quietly out of the doorway. She couldn't have it now. She'd given the police a dummy thermos and somehow hidden the real one. The one from which she'd just served unusually hot V-8 juice.

I massaged my burning stomach. Melinda had poured herself some V-8, too, but she'd taken only the barest sip. She'd been talking; it had seemed natural for her to ignore her drink.

And I, interested in her gossip, had downed the whole spicy cupful.

I had to get myself down to basement first-aid. My throat was on fire. I couldn't swallow. My nose and eyes were running.

I turned around and took a few shaky steps. I heard Melinda call out, "Willa!"

"Ladies' room! Right back!" I said, moving faster.

I'd seen it in her time and time again: a passion to keep the office together. And killing LeVoq had been the only sure way. But she'd done it too late. LeVoq had already arranged for Aasgar to leave. Office warfare had already driven the baby lawyers away.

Then I'd started asking questions about Bud Hopper; looked a gift horse in the mouth. I'd asked Mott point-blank if he'd ever talked to Hopper. It was an unwitting accusation: whoever told him Hopper wanted me at the retreat was lying.

And Mott put two and two together. Melinda had relayed "Hopper's" request. My presence at the retreat made me a murder suspect. And Melinda had hated LeVoq enough to kill him.

Mott responded by pulling Melinda off her biggest case, World Financial. Lovers or not, if he suspected her of wrongdoing, his first move would be to protect the law firm.

Melinda was savvy enough to interpret the action correctly. Mott had guessed the truth. So Mott had died, too.

And now it was my turn. Maybe the original plan had been to kill LeVoq, with suspicion falling on me or on some untraceable psychopath bent on copying the Warneke murder. Either way, had things worked out, I'd have left the firm under a cloud of (unprovable) suspicion; and the San Francisco office would have been saved.

But the unplanned, unavoidable (from her point of view) murder of William Mott changed everything. It narrowed the field of suspects. Narrowed it to someone in the office.

If I died of hemlock poisoning, maybe the police would believe it was suicide—in remorse for murder. A bit of hemlock smeared on the cutting board of the house where I'd been staying, and the stage was set.

But I had to die. As long as I was alive the inquiry would continue. That was bad for business. It had nearly cost Melinda her partnership.

Maybe she'd even typed a suicide note for me.

I tried to walk faster.

My eyes were streaming. I could hardly see. Krisbaum said the stuff acted quickly on me. And I hadn't eaten since last night's cold hominy.

"Willa!" Melinda's voice, sharper.

If I could just get downstairs to the first aid station.

But the next thing I knew Melinda was standing in front of me, blocking my path.

I gasped, taking a staggering step backward.

She knew I'd guessed. And she made it plain I'd guessed right.

She knocked me down.

43

IF SHE COULD keep me down for a short while, we both knew I wouldn't get up again.

She sat on me, pressing my shoulders to the floor. I tried to flail at her, but couldn't raise my arms high enough to do her any harm. In my panic, I smashed my hand against McNee's desk; pain jangled up my arm.

It was hard to breathe. I had a hammering headache, and my chest muscles were tightening. How did hemlock kill? Why hadn't I asked the nurses how it killed? Paralysis of the lungs? I tried to draw a breath. Relax,

relax. She's on your diaphragm; that's why you can't breathe.

I blinked tears away. Couldn't seem to control them; as if I'd bitten peppers.

I looked up at her. Maybe she was joking. We were friends, weren't we?

Her hair was disheveled, her face was very white; she looked scared. A strand of hair was in her mouth, another tickled her nose. If she'd let go of my arm to brush it away—

I felt her stiffen. Her weight on my diaphragm increased. The phone rang, six or seven feet away, at the far end of McNee's desk. It rang again, an electronic warble. She was staring at it. I drew up my knees. If I could catch her off guard . . .

It warbled again. Someone had asked the answering service to ring through.

Melinda was too far up my torso for me to kick. Maybe I could push her off with my knee. I saw a jolt of surprise in her eyes as my knee nudged the small of her back—far too gently.

The phone was still ringing. If I could knock her off balance and get to it—I tried again to sit up. To move my arms. To buck her off.

Melinda was six inches taller and maybe forty pounds heavier than me. But that wasn't the whole problem. My adrenaline should have compensated.

She was as scared as I was. I could feel it in her grip, see it in her crumpled face. Her adrenaline was pumping too.

If I got away from her now, I'd tell the world she'd tried to kill me. Tried twice. She'd poisoned the dregs of the Bloody Mary yesterday. Then she'd hidden the thermos and given the police a substitute.

The phone stopped, midring. Damn. I ceased struggling; could hardly breathe.

Melinda's grip tightened.

I tried to get one good breath. A good look at the woman I'd thought was my friend.

Her boss had been about to steal the firm's sustaining client and open his own law office; blithely knocking out the underpinnings of her career.

And suddenly the newspapers began running long articles about hemlock: what it looked like, where to find it, tips on fatal dosage. Julian Warneke's murder had made hemlock a hot topic.

If she could just feed some to Bob LeVoq, she could save the office, and salvage her painfully built career. Except that after years of office friction, she'd be the obvious suspect.

The idea taking shape: Get someone from the Warneke firm to work at Wailes, Roth. The police would suspect that person. Or they'd suspect some crazy copycat murderer, inspired by the Warneke lawyer's presence.

But Julian's partners already had new jobs. That left only me, a relative novice from a not-quite-top-drawer law school. It would take an impressive recommendation to overcome the deficiencies in my résumé. It would take research: Finding someone on the verge of leaving a prestigious job for some faraway place—a place like South Africa. Finding something I'd done that might plausibly attract his notice. My student law review article; the partners might check to make sure it existed, but they wouldn't bother reading it.

A couple of phone calls. Melinda had a deep voice, almost androgynous. Deepen it a little, add a hint of snobbery, a few D.C. anecdotes—Melinda had gone to law school there; it wouldn't take much to pull off the masquerade. After that, she could lobby openly for hiring me. She could urge Mott to recommend me to the L.A. partners: as she put it, the firm needed another body.

All that remained was to choose the time and place

for LeVoq's murder. The Mariposa retreat was perfect—there were plenty of outsiders spicing the stew: clients, spouses, lovers, strangers. And LeVoq had been ordered not to come—a dare he'd never refuse.

Getting me invited must have been easy: Tell Mott some partner or other had passed along a request from Hopper, and Mott would have to oblige. And if I hadn't made such a fuss about him, who would have given Hopper a second thought? Who would have connected the fictional request to LeVoq's murder?

But as things turned out, Mott did give it a second thought. He wondered if Hopper *was* a pretext, after all. He talked to the partner who'd supposedly been in touch with him. And he came to the conclusion that Melinda had invented Hopper.

He realized what it meant. And realized he'd better reassign Melinda's cases, before anyone else found out. He had no choice but to give me the Malhousie case— I was the only lawyer left in San Francisco.

The reassignment protected the firm—but it also announced Mott's revelation to Melinda.

She hadn't managed to save the office, but she could still save herself. She could kill William Mott.

No question of blaming an anonymous copycat for this one, nor even a jealous wife or girlfriend (that's why she'd taken the picture of LeVoq in my room: add to the suspects, shift attention away from a business motive). She'd have to blame me.

She was smart enough to see what Krisbaum would think: that I was sick, that I was making a neurotic bid for attention.

But as long as I lived, I was walking proof of my own sanity. If, on the other hand, I died of hemlock poisoning . . . The police would conclude I'd killed myself in remorse.

Krisbaum would.

I stared up at her, shaking my head. My throat felt

blistered, my mouth swollen; I couldn't speak. I couldn't tell her Surgelato wouldn't believe it. Couldn't tell her the police had arrested Justin Poat; that if she'd left things alone, the cops would have settled for him.

But if they found me dead now, with nothing but tomato juice in my stomach, they'd turn their attention to her.

She was right to look scared. She was doomed.

And if she sat on me much longer, so was I.

The phone rang again. She jerked her hands back, momentarily yanking my arms off the carpet. She craned her neck to look at the phone, up on McNee's desk. It rang. Rang again.

I wriggled. Tried again to kick. Reporters? I thought of my reporter friend, Manuel Boyd, dead of AIDS. I'd go quickly at least, wouldn't I?

I tried to summon up a surge of adrenaline. But I knew it wouldn't match hers. I was too sick to fight. Almost too sick to want to try.

In a way it would be a relief. Maybe she'd ease off my diaphragm when I stopped thrashing. Maybe I could get that one big breath.

Or maybe she'd think I was playing possum.

Playing possum. I forced my legs to jerk. Three, four, five big spasms. The phone was still trilling.

I lowered my eyelids as if I couldn't keep them up, then twitched my eyes open. I let my mouth hang, feeling myself drool. I flung my arms as powerfully as I could, once again smacking my knuckles on McNee's desk.

Melinda stared at me in wide-eyed horror, mouth drawn back in a panting moan. It was working: she thought she was watching me die. Maybe she was.

More drooling; I couldn't help it. My eyes closed. A few more jerks. Then I went limp.

The phone stopped ringing. It was quiet in the office. Just the sound of my heart hammering, a roaring in my eardrums. Melinda was still panting, making a keening sound deep in her throat. Her grip was still tight.

The pain in my chest was fading; it felt like butterflies now. I'm slipping away, I thought. No need to pretend.

And then finally, I felt her weight shift off my torso onto her knees. Her hands clamped tighter, then looser on my arms. She was trying to decide if I was gone.

Mother. Daddy. Came to me with a bomb-the-bank poster when I got out of jail. The poster was stupid, but I didn't care. You came. You were there. You were waiting. That's what I remember.

The phone again. It startled me. I opened my eyes. Thank god she didn't notice.

She stared at the phone, grip loosened, weight shifted. And provided me the edge I needed. I took that big breath.

And I gave it all I had.

I sat up, snapping my arms free. I pushed her off balance, then dived sideways, arms extended. I grabbed for the telephone cord and yanked the whole mass of glowing buttons off McNee's desk. I managed two hoarse words as the receiver tumbled from the cradle.

''Help me!''

Then I watched Melinda's hand hit the disconnect button.

She was on me like an avalanche before I passed out.

44

I OPENED MY eyes. A glint of light off something close: a chrome rail. A plastic box with levers and diagrams of beds folding and flattening. Beyond that, a nightstand with a bowl, a box of tissue, and a dirty tote bag inscribed *Stop Acid Rain*.

In a chair, my mother, wiping her eyes.

She looked at me. Her face changed: despair to delight, just like that.

"Baby!" She leaned over the bed, brushing hair out of my face. "I was so scared!" She didn't have to tell me. It was still in her eyes. "I love you." She didn't have to tell me that, either.

I fumbled for her cold, wrinkled hand.

There were tubes in my arm. "Do the bed for me."

She didn't bother wiping away tears now. They were coming too fast. She pressed the lever that raised the pillow end of the bed.

"Was that you on the phone?"

She nodded. "I was scared, Willa. That you'd really

leave us." She plumbed her tote bag for a wad of tissue, savagely wiping her nose. "I was ashamed of myself."

"Me too."

She blinked at me, hesitating. "I knew you were at your office because Stanley, the boy I sent over, said you were. But when I called, you didn't answer. I let it ring and ring, but you didn't answer." She leaned close enough for me to smell cold cream and incense. "And you see, I *knew* it wasn't Justin! I knew *he* didn't give you the hemlock. And if it wasn't him, then the killer was still out there!"

Justin Poat. It made no difference that he was innocent. The cops had scared him and he'd struggled with them. He'd violated his parole. He'd be shipped back to Soledad. "Oh, Mother! I'm sorry about Justin!"

We locked hands in mute, helpless pity for the man.

Then falteringly, she continued. "The second time I phoned, I got scared. I thought maybe the killer was there with you, in your office with you. So I called that lieutenant."

"Don? You called Don Surgelato?"

She nodded. "And he phoned your office. He found out you were in trouble."

Looking at her ashen cheeks and frightened eyes, I was glad she hadn't heard my croaking plea for help.

"He called building security and the first-aid people. He told them to rush upstairs—Oh, baby!" She raised my hand to her wet cheek. "They pumped your stomach on the spot, but they thought for a while it might be too late. That you'd taken too much into your system. If you didn't wake up soon, they were going to try transfusions! Daddy's still downstairs giving blood."

My mouth was cottony and my neck was wracked with cricks. My ribs ached and my stomach was jumpy, to say the least. The room was overly bright for my tired eyes. But it really wasn't too bad. Only a little worse than waking up after a day-long acid trip (if I remembered correctly after—my god!—fifteen years).

I looked at Mother. We didn't agree on the fine points of liberal politics any more. I didn't care. She didn't look like she did, either.

When Don Surgelato walked in, we were cheek to cheek, crying.

45

HER FIRST WORDS to him were, "What are you going to do about Justin Poat?"

He glanced at me anxiously. I must have looked awful. I wiped tears away with a corner of my bedsheet. He turned to Mother.

In the afternoon light, his face looked pale and tired. It was OK Corral time. Whatever he said to Mother now would haunt all three of us. "I made a mistake," he admitted. "I'll tell the parole board that."

A twinge of hope crossed Mother's face. "Will it make a difference?"

"No. He struck a police officer."

"But he wouldn't have done it if you hadn't—"

"I know that! But our system of justice requires him to take responsibility for his action—regardless of what triggered it!"

There were a great many things Mother could have said in response. I'd heard them all a hundred times. The quality of mercy. A victim of circumstance. The crime of punishment. Judge not lest ye be judged.

She stood frowning, watching him.

She had organized a campaign to hold Surgelato accountable for shooting Julian Warneke's killer. She'd shown him no mercy; cared nothing for circumstance.

I looked at Surgelato. His brows were pinched and his jaw muscles rippled. Follow-up investigations might result in official censure: censure of conduct engaged in for Mother's benefit.

Nothing either of them could say, really.

I broke the silence. "Mother, could you go find me a nurse?"

She sighed, relaxing her shoulders. Then she nodded, walking past Surgelato without looking at him.

He expelled his breath when the door closed behind her.

I said, "Thank you." And managed to smile.

He moistened his lips, took a quick stride across the room and bent over me, smoothing my hair. His suit jacket was open; I could see a shoulder holster strapped under his arm.

He kissed me.

I'd miss him, in L.A.

About the Author

Lia Matera is a graduate of Hastings College of Law, where she was editor of the *Constitutional Law Review*. She was later a teaching fellow at Stanford Law School. Since 1987 she has been a critically acclaimed mystery writer. *Where Lawyers Fear to Tread* was her debut—and also the launch for one of her series heroines: Willa Jansson. The novel was nominated for an Anthony Award, and its sequel, *A Radical Departure*, was nominated for both an Anthony and an Edgar Allan Poe Award. Subsequent novels include *The Smart Money* (the debut of Laura Di Palma), *Hidden Agenda*, *The Good Fight*, and *Prior Convictions*. Ms. Matera lives in Santa Cruz, California, with her son.